Elgar's 'Enigma' Variations

– a centenary celebration

PATRICK TURNER

Thames Publishing
London

Elgar dedicated his Op 36 *Variations* 'to my friends pictured within'.

This study is wholly concerned with the *Variations*, and so it seems appropriate to continue the idea of paying tribute to friends.

I therefore dedicate this book, with love and grateful thanks, to:

Michael Ullmann

... who knows little about music and less about Elgar
but much about friendship.

How I wonder what you are . . .

(Nursery Rhyme)

Contents

Acknowledgements

Although it has many advantages as a place to live, Barcelona is not the most convenient place to be when researching anything to do with Elgar.

For this reason my first expression of gratitude must go to those who, through their thorough researches over the years, have paved the way and thus made life considerably easier for all those of us who follow, and in particular to Michael Kennedy, Jerrold Northrop Moore and Percy Young.

My geographical location has also meant that part of my researches has had to be conducted by post. I am grateful to all those who patiently responded to my requests for information, in particular Chris Bennett at the Elgar Birthplace, Peter Whidden at Stanford University, Claire Orr at the Hereford and Worcester Record Office, Mick Wood of the National Meteorological Library and Archive, Brigitte Winsor of Birmingham Central Library, Alison Cooper of Sheffield Central Library, Richard Bond of Manchester Central Library, my uncle Fred Druce, local historian in Ross-on-Wye, Dr John Jones of Balliol College, Oxford, Susan Marshall of Exeter College, Oxford, James Strebing, timpanist with the City of Birmingham Symphony Orchestra, and Geoff and Gill Bradshaw and Hywel Davies of the West Midlands Branch of the Elgar Society. Grateful thanks also to my daughter Catherine, who undertook various errands for me in London.

I owe a special word of thanks to Robert Anderson, who found time to chat with me during a rare visit of his to Barcelona. Thanks also are due to my sister Jane Fallon, who was kind enough to read the text with a very unsisterly eye to check it out for clarity. Barry Collett also did me the honour of checking through the text, and both his and my sister's valuable input have undoubtedly improved the book, although clearly any nonsenses which may remain are solely my responsibility.

Two final words of thanks. As an innocent abroad in the world of publishing, I am indebted to John Bishop and John Saunders of Thames Publishing for their patient help and guidance. I should also acknowledge my mother's contribution to the book, as without her constant badgering that I should get my ideas down on paper, I am not sure that I would ever have embarked on the project.

Any undertaking such as this one is inevitably time-consuming and so I am grateful to my family for their infinite patience and unfailing support and encouragement.

*   *   *

The publisher wishes to thank the Trustees of the Elgar Birthplace, the Trustees of the Elgar Will Trust, the British Library, Raymond Monk, Mrs Iliffe, Mrs Mary Fraser and E A Butcher for permission to use photographs. In some cases it has been impossible to establish copyright ownership.

A Note on the Notes

In my experience footnotes tend to get in the way of the flow of the text one is reading. For this reason, I have grouped mine at the end of each chapter, and, within the constrictions imposed by the need to clearly identify my sources, I have tried to keep them as few and as simple as possible.

The reader will find, therefore, that there are no comments or related points made in the notes, these being reserved exclusively for identification of sources. They can thus be quite happily ignored altogether unless the reader wishes to check the origin of some quotation or other.

Published works are referred to in as brief a way as possible consistent with clarity. For example, Mrs Richard Powell's book *Memories of a Variation* is referred to simply as 'Powell', followed by the appropriate page number. Full details of this and other published sources can be found in the bibliography.

As far as the letters are concerned, in cases where I have quoted from one of the published collections, I give the reference of that collection. In cases where I have quoted directly from the letters themselves I give the location and reference number of the actual document.

Abbreviations used are as follows:

HWRO	Hereford and Worcester Record Office
ESN	*Elgar Society Newsletter*
ESJ	*Elgar Society Journal*

These last two refer to the same publication, the denomination 'Journal' having been adopted as from the Jan 1979 issue. The originals of Alice Elgar's diaries I consulted are held in the Barber Fine Art and Music Library of the University of Birmingham.

I have not individually annotated each reference. Readers may be interested to know that facsimile copies of the diaries are held at the Hereford and Worcester Record Office and at the Elgar Birthplace, whilst a typescript of them by Jerrold Northrop Moore is held in the British Library.

Introduction

The enigma of Elgar's *'Enigma' Variations* is far and away the best-known puzzle in English music and is very probably unique in the whole of music. What is the hidden theme that goes with the theme of Elgar's variations? Is it a musical or an abstract theme? Was there a hidden theme at all?

These questions have intrigued lovers of Elgar's music, and indeed lovers of music in general, ever since the work was first performed in 1899, but to date no completely satisfactory solution has been found, which only serves to make the whole matter even more tantalising.

That the matter is of general interest is clear from the fact that whenever a particularly interesting idea is put forward, it prompts articles in the national press, for instance in *The Daily Telegraph* of 18 June 1986 and *The Sunday Telegraph* of 3 November 1991.

However, the question of the hidden theme is by no means the only puzzling thing about Elgar's Op 36 *Variations*; indeed, the work is surrounded by a veritable constellation of intriguing aspects and question marks, much more so than any of his other works, and not surprisingly this fact has given rise to a plethora of theories, a lot of which can only be described as fanciful.

Indeed, so much ink has been devoted to the *'Enigma' Variations* that one can almost hear dear old Sir Edward grumbling...

I wish people wd. drown themselves in ink & let me alone.

... as he did once towards the end of his life in a letter to his daughter Carice[1].

Clearly, by taking up my own pen, I too am risking the wrath of Elgar's shade. But at the same time, as I put the finishing touches to this book it is a hundred years to the day since the October evening in 1898 when Elgar, 'soothed and feeling rested', sat down at the piano and began to play and so set the hare running.

It seemed to me that this centenary was a good time for synthesis. A good time for re-appraising all the various elements that have survived and drawing conclusions firmly based on them.

What I have tried to do in this study is look at the various issues raised by the Op 36 *Variations* in the light of all the available evidence we have at our disposal. 'Evidence', in fact, is a word which occurs with a frequency which I hope the reader will not find annoying.

However, as is natural in any search for what actually happened, I have also set forth various hypotheses, but in all cases these, as any hypothesis should, not only respect the available evidence but also provide plausible explanation for otherwise obscure or inexplicable points.

What the reader will emphatically not find in what follows is the sort of hopeless nonsense such as can be found in one article on the subject, whose author, in search of clues to connect the *Variations* and Alexander Pope, suggested that at one point in the score Elgar concealed the name 'Pope' upside down in the horn part.

As Garry Humphreys put it in a letter in the September 1984 issue of the *Elgar Society Journal*, '... sometimes I think we try just too hard!'

Whatever the judgement on the ideas set out in this study, I sincerely hope that it will not be said that I have tried too hard.

Barcelona
21 October 1998

Notes

1. Moore – *Lifetime Letters* – p 458

12

Introduction To
Second Edition

Seeing my book go into a second edition is a source of great satisfaction, the more so because it coincides with the year that sees the 150th anniversary of Elgar's birth. The book was greeted very favourably when it first appeared eight years ago. The Elgar Society website called it 'the clearest, best researched volume on this subject yet published'; whilst the review in the 12 June 1999 edition of Classical Music said 'Turner's account (is) the one which will best enhance the general reader's appreciation of a much-loved work.' And my comment in the original introduction to the effect that new ideas about this work prompt articles in the national press was proved accurate by the article about the book that appeared in The Observer on 14 February 1999. I was also interviewed on the BBC's Today programme.

However, gratifying as all this was, the comment that went straight to my heart was one made in a letter to me by Raymond Monk, a prominent figure in Elgar scholarship. He said of my book 'Carice Elgar would have been delighted with it, I'm absolutely sure about that.'

In the period since the book was published, no new evidence has come to light that would cause me to modify any of the conclusions I reached when I wrote it. Accordingly, the original text is maintained in this edition, with the exception of the correction of one or two spelling mistakes that crept into the original version. One of these was particularly unfortunate. It is always embarrassing to get someone's name wrong, and I feel particularly bad about this one, as of all the orchestral timpanists I wrote to (about half a dozen), James Strebing of the City of Birmingham Symphony Orchestra was the only one who took the trouble to reply. His letter and our subsequent phone conversation were invaluable to me in writing the section about the timpani part in Variation XIII. I hope he will accept my apologies.

I have added one new chapter, which follows the original text. This reflects comments that have been made to me, or articles that have been written on the subject, since the book's first publication. Part of this is an update on recordings of the work made since 1999. I am again grateful to John Knowles for making available to me his monumental database on all recordings of Elgar's works.

One final word. The book's first publisher, Thames Publishing, literally was John Bishop. John's publishing activities were totally dedicated to British music, and when he died in 2000, Trevor Hold's tribute to him said this: 'in his passing, British music - composers, performers and listeners - have lost a stalwart, indefatigable champion.' It gives me pleasure to reflect that his memory lives on in the books he published, and in new editions of them such as this one.

Singapore
17 January 2007

The Variations

Dedicated to my Friends Pictured Within

Variation	Title	Identity
Theme	Enigma	
I	C.A.E.	Alice Elgar
II	H.D.S.-P	Hew Steuart Powell
III	R.B.T.	Richard Baxter Townshend
IV	W.M.B.	William Meath Baker
V	R.P.A.	Richard Penrose Arnold
VI	Ysobel	Isabel Fitton
VII	Troyte	Arthur Troyte Griffith
VIII	W.N.	Winifred Norbury
IX	Nimrod	August Jaeger
X	Dorabella (Intermezzo)	Dora Penny
XI	G.R.S.	George Sinclair
XII	B.G.N.	Basil Nevinson
XIII	***(Romanza)	Lady Mary Lygon
XIV	E.D.U. (Finale)	Elgar

1 – The Origins

The birth of the Variations

The first thing to be said, and it is a key point, is that in the beginning there was no enigma in the sense that we now understand it.

Both J A Forsyth in 1932 and Basil Maine the following year give broadly similar accounts of the evening the *Variations* were born. Elgar returned home, a house called 'Forli' in Malvern, after a day giving violin lessons, and, after dinner, settled down at the piano with a cigar. It was almost certainly the evening of 21 October 1898 as that day was a Friday, Elgar's normal day for teaching at 'The Mount', a school in Malvern run by Rosa Burley:

> I musingly played on the piano the theme as it now stands. The voice of
> C.A.E. [Alice Elgar – his wife] asked with a sound of approval
>   'What is that?'
> I answered 'Nothing – but something might be made of it...'[1]

He then played different versions of the theme as various friends might have interpreted it, even inviting his wife to guess the identity of some of the friends involved.

Forsyth and Maine, it is true, were writing long after the event but their accounts correspond with newspaper reports dating from before the first performance. For example. *The Sheffield Independent* of 12 June 1899 states:

> It happened that he [Elgar] was extemporising on the pianoforte one
> evening, and 'chanced on' a pleasing theme. Turning to a friend in the
> room he remarked that a certain person would play the melody in a
> particular way, that somebody else would play it differently...[2]

It is worth mentioning that Alice Elgar's diary says nothing at all about any of this; in fact her first mention of the *Variations* does not occur until 25 January 1899, when Elgar was busy with their orchestration. The first mention of the *Variations* in Elgar's letters occurs in a letter to August Jaeger of the London music publishing firm Novello. Jaeger, as well as being Elgar's main contact at Novello, was a close friend who was to be immortalised in the 'Nimrod' variation. In this letter, dated 24 October 1898, we can see that in three days the idea had snowballed:

> Since I've been back I have sketched a set of Variations (orkestra) on an original theme: the Variations have amused me because I've labelled 'em with the nicknames of my particular friends - you are Nimrod: That is to say I've written the variations each one to represent the mood of the 'party' – I've liked to imagine the 'party' writing the var:him (or her) self & have written what I think they wd. have written – if they were asses enough to compose...[3]

This letter would indicate that the whole work was clear in Elgar's head and indeed physically existed in the form of sketches, and that he already saw it as orchestral: all this barely 72 hours after the first emergence of the theme on the piano.

Elgar had returned to Malvern from London on 19 October, as can be clearly seen from his letter to Jaeger dated 20 October:

> only arrd. last night...[4]

This letter is full of the familiar Elgar complaints that his music didn't pay and that there was no point going on:

> ...I tell you I am sick of it all...

The tone of the 24 October letter is completely different and shows Elgar in a far more cheerful state of mind. It seems clear that it was the birth of the *Variations* which restored Elgar's good humour, quite simply because the news of the *Variations* sketches is the main reason for writing, the rest of the letter consisting of a couple of short sentences hoping that Jaeger's house-hunting was going well and commenting on how the local woods were looking.

Confirmation of this comes from Elgar himself writing some years later, when he said that the work was commenced...

...in a spirit of humour.[5]

Further confirmation comes from Rosa Burley when she describes Elgar's next visit to 'The Mount' on 28 October:

> He came to The Mount in the rather excited state which usually indicated some new inspiration...[6]

Yet further confirmation comes from Dora Penny (the 'Dorabella' of Variation X), who visited the Elgars the following week (1 November) and heard some of the variations played by Elgar on the piano. She tells us that...

> the composer was in high spirits.[7]

What transpires from all this is that in the very beginning the *Variations* were fun for Elgar and through him to the people immediately around him.

What is also evident is that Elgar just like anybody fired by a new enthusiasm, developed the *Variations* very quickly over the first ten days of their existence.

As can be seen in the 24 October letter to Jaeger, a 'Nimrod' variation is already being talked about. Dorabella, as I will call her from here on, mentions hearing six variations (including 'Nimrod') on her 1 November visit, but she doesn't mention either Steuart Powell or Nevinson, who, if we believe Elgar as reported by Maine, were the first two attempts.

Counting all this up, we have specific references to eight of the fourteen variations in their first ten days or so of life.

But we have not one single reference to an enigma of any kind. Which can only mean that the fundamental underlying drive behind those immensely creative days was constituted by the variations themselves and not by any enigma solely concerning the theme. This would seem to be confirmed by an early sketch of it which just has the word 'Theme' written above the music with no mention of the word 'enigma'.

The theme is mentioned in various accounts, for example by Rosa Burley:

...wistful but hardly of outstanding interest...[8]

or Dorabella:

...a very odd tune...[9]

but there is never any hint or suggestion of anything else behind. Rosa Burley is explicit on this point:

He was far more concerned with the variations than with the underlying theme and constantly challenged me to guess whom they represented.[10]

Taking all the foregoing into account, it seems to me that what might appear to be a surprising conclusion can be drawn: the driving force behind the *Variations* was the aspect of musical portraiture or caricature, starting off from a sort of family joke (although already by 24 October Elgar was talking of having developed the *Variations* as a set for orchestra.)

Nobody in those early days was being told anything about hidden themes – they were simply being challenged to guess the identity of each variation. From which we can conclude that the possible existence of any such hidden theme was not judged to be of importance. Part of the fun in setting a puzzle is watching people trying to solve it, as indeed Elgar was doing with the variations. Had there been a deliberate puzzle concerning the theme, he would surely have acted in exactly the same way. The fact that he wasn't doing this would suggest that the whole question of the 'enigma' as a hidden theme was not a conscious aspect of the genesis of the work.

Or, put another way, the whole question of the hidden theme was not a deliberately created puzzle on Elgar's part. This is clearly a very important point, the implications of which I will return to in Chapter 3. As has already been noted, the early development of the *Variations* was extremely rapid. This speed was maintained throughout, for the orchestral score was completed on 19 February 1899, less than four months after the original idea for the work. The orchestration itself was done in two weeks – the equivalent of one variation every day.

And of course, while work on the *Variations* was progressing, Elgar was involved in a multitude of other things: revisions to the *Froissart* score, checking material for analytical notes on *King Olaf*, various bits of business concerning various music festivals, a bout of depression near Christmas (this seemed to happen to Elgar most years), two trips to London during which he saw Jaeger, and so on.

It is obvious that the *Variations* must have been occupying a great deal of Elgar's time and thoughts during this period and yet there are no references to them in Alice's diary and very few references to them in Elgar's letters. In November, he wrote to Jaeger:

The Variations go on slowly but I shall finish 'em some day[11]

In January 1899 came two references in two days, the first to Jaeger:

I say – those variations – I like 'em.[12]

...and the second to his friend, Nicholas Kilburn:

I have completed nearly a set of Variations for orchestra which I like - but commercially nothing[13]

The first of the trips to London took place between 9 and 17 January 1899 and it would have been during this stay that Elgar first had the opportunity to talk with Jaeger about the *Variations* and play over the music to him, although curiously, when Elgar sent the score of the piano arrangement of the *Variations* to Jaeger on 13 March, he commented in his covering letter:

Mrs. J. will recognize your portrait quicker than you will... [14]

suggesting that Jaeger was not already familiar with it.

It was also during this stay that the idea of approaching the renowned conductor Hans Richter to conduct the first performance surfaced. Whether the idea was Jaeger's, Nathaniel Vert's (Richter's agent) or Elgar's own will be discussed later, but it was clearly agreed that Elgar should send the completed score as soon as possible to Vert for onward transmission to Richter, for as soon as Elgar got back home he worked frenetically to get his work finished and orchestrated.

On 16 February, three days before the scoring was completed, he wrote to FG Edwards, Editor of the *Musical Times*, announcing the new work:

> Just completed a set of Symphonic Variations (theme original) for orchestra... [15]

Two days after it was finished, the manuscript full score was sent to Vert, who replied the following day telling Elgar that he was going to forward it with a covering letter to Richter that very evening.

That score is now in the British Library and has the word 'Enigma' in pencil over the theme. But that single word is not in Elgar's handwriting and it therefore seems safe to assume that it was not on the score when it was sent to Vert.

As at that point, then, with the work completed and despatched to its future first conductor, there is still absolutely no evidence whatsoever of any enigma. No mention anywhere in letters or memoirs, sketches or even the score itself of the puzzle which was to attach itself to this work.

It is indeed curious to observe that the enigma which has fascinated so many people over the years, and which has come to designate the work itself (we talk of the *'Enigma' Variations* whereas at no time did Elgar use this nomenclature), is so totally absent from all the surviving records covering the four months of its gestation.

Before moving on, one of the early sketches of the Op 36 *Variations* should be mentioned. This particular sketch has the comment 'to be critikised' in Elgar's handwriting, and as it was found interleaved in Jaeger's copy of the score, the conclusion has been drawn that Elgar sent this sketch to Jaeger at an early stage of development of the work, in search of his opinion.

This has always seemed to me implausible as there is absolutely no mention of the sketch in any of the surviving letters of the period, and in any case Elgar was not in the habit of asking Jaeger's (or anyone else's for that matter) critical opinion on something so fundamentally important as would have been the theme of the *Variations*. True, Elgar did occasionally send Jaeger one or two bars of music for him to look at, but never in the way suggested by the comment on this sketch. It is also true that Jaeger made many critical comments on parts of Elgar's scores (most notably in the case of *The Dream of Gerontius*), but in all these cases they were spontaneous comments which not only did not respond to any request from the composer but which most of the time met with resistance on the part of this latter. In the case of *Caractacus*, the work immediately preceding the *Variations*, Elgar even went so far as to ask Jaeger not to make any comment:

> May I thank you for not saying one word about the work, either for or against & please don't YET or I shall surely die, being on edge.[16]

And this was written just four-and-a-half months before the theme of the *Variations* emerged on Elgar's piano.

So what alternative explanation might there be? Some clues are furnished by the sketch itself. For example, it is dated October 1898. Now it was not Elgar's normal practise to date his sketches unless he made gifts of them at a later date, in which case he wrote on the sketch the date, or approximate date, of its writing. To quote just one example, in 1909 he gave his friend Ivor Atkins, who was organist at Worcester Cathedral, a sketch of the First Symphony dating from the year before and duly dated 1908.[17] This would therefore suggest that the sketch was given to Jaeger some time after it was actually written.

This possibility is supported by another clue to be found in the sketch, this time in the peculiar spelling of the word 'critikise' using a 'k'. Elgar loved word-games, plays on words and puns of all kinds, and frequently a particular word or phrase would lodge itself in his mind for a period of time. His letters reflect this, and it is thus of particular relevance that the only time in all his surviving correspondence to Jaeger that the word 'criticise' occurs spelled with a 'k' is in a letter dated 28 August 1901.[18] One of Jaeger's letters to Elgar, dated 19 February 1903, has the same spelling.[19] On the other hand, the same word is used in a letter to Jaeger dated early September 1898, ie, just before the *Variations* were conceived, but this time spelled normally.[20] This would thus suggest that the comment on the sketch in question, with the word 'critikise' spelled with a 'k', does not date from the same period as the sketch itself.

As to when the comment might have been added, another of Elgar's letters to Jaeger provides a plausible answer. In his letter of 13 November 1901 (thus dating from the same period as the 28 August letter referred to above) Elgar says the following:

If I tear things –1st sketches I mean–up you say I'm a fool. If I send 'em to you you say I'm a conceited ass. So I send you one or two scraps–if you do not want 'em my little wife does.[21]

Of course it is impossible to be sure, but it seems unlikely that the scraps in question were first sketches of *The Dream of Gerontius* as Elgar had already sent Jaeger what he said were the 'very first' sketches of this work in September 1900.[22] And as at the time of this letter, apart from *The Dream of Gerontius*, Op 38, none of Elgar's other works since the Op 36 *Variations* (*Sea Pictures*, Op 37, the first two *Pomp and Circumstance Marches*, Op 39, *Cockaigne*, Op 40, *Two Songs*, Op 41) had been published by Jaeger's firm, Novello, it seems reasonable to surmise that the scraps in question could well have been the first sketches of the *Variations*.

If this is indeed the case, the comment 'to be critikised' can be easily understood as a friendly ironic challenge, given Jaeger's outspoken comments on some aspects of the original version of *The Dream of Gerontius* on the one hand, and the outstanding success of the *Variations* on the other.

The birth of the Enigma

Vert sent the manuscript orchestral score to Richter in Vienna while Elgar crossed his fingers and hoped for the best. Meanwhile, news of the work started to appear in the press. F G Edwards, on the basis of Elgar's letter quoted above, duly wrote a piece for the *Musical Times*, and picking up on this, J A Betts, the musical correspondent of *The Daily News*, dedicated a paragraph to Elgar and the *Variations* in the issue of Friday 24 February, just three days after the manuscript score had been sent to Vert. Betts wrote thus:

> For a London concert in the spring Mr. Elgar has, for example, written fourteen orchestral 'Symphonic Variations', intended, it is said, as sketch portraits of his friends, or rather he 'has looked at the theme through the personality, if not the spectacles, of thirteen other men and women.' The idea opens up infinite possibilities. An orchestral portrait of Professor Bridge by Professor Stanford – and vice versa – would, for example, be especially interesting.

This last comment clearly appealed to Elgar's sense of fun as well as to his dislike and distrust of the London musical establishment as personified in Frederick Bridge and Charles Stanford, teachers of composition at the Royal College of Music. He commented on it in two of his letters the day after the article appeared, one of them to Jaeger:

> I could not think where that pig Betts got his yarn from on Friday & his wicked joke.[23]

And yet the thought of the London musical establishment and perhaps also the fact that the *Variations* were now being talked about publicly with specific mention of a spring first performance in London, whereas nothing of the sort was anywhere near finalisation, prompted a sudden nervousness with regard to the fate of the score, by now on its way to Vienna. In the same letter to Jaeger Elgar says:

> ... for mercy's sake don't tell <u>anyone</u> I pray you about Richter – becos' he may refuse...

A little later in the same letter he says:

> ... I fear R. has been 'got at'.

The same day he wrote to Dorabella:

> He, R., is to see 'em [the *Variations*] in Vienna very soon and – <u>if he is not prevented by certain London – (mystery!)</u> will play you all in the Spring...[24]

However, there was nothing he could do except busy himself with other things, one of which was completing the piano arrangement of the *Variations* which was sent to Novello on 13 March.

This score, now in the possession of Stanford University, has no mention of the word 'enigma', and this would tend to confirm that the orchestral score sent to Richter via Vert did not at that stage have any mention of the word either.

Richter eventually signalled his agreement to conduct the first performance and this news was duly relayed by Elgar in letters to Ivor Atkins (24 March)[25] and Dorabella (26 March)[26]. It was also relayed, although not by Elgar himself, to Charles Ainslie Barry, composer and writer on music, who was usually entrusted with the task of writing the programme notes for Richter's concerts. Barry contacted Elgar in search of background information and it is in his first letter, dated 10 April 1899, that we find the first surviving reference to an enigma in connection with the *Variations*.

In this letter, Barry says that he has been told that Richter had agreed to conduct the first performance and that he (Barry) was to be responsible for writing the programme notes. He refers to some Variations written by himself some thirty years earlier in which there was a 'trick' of some kind, and continues:

> You won't guess it, so I am glad to think that there is something
> enigmatical about my Variations, as well as your's [sic].[27]

On 30 April Barry wrote again:

> Novellos have sent me proof sheets (...) of your Enigma (which I cannot
> guess) and Variations.[28]

This is fascinating, for given the context and his use of capital
letters, Barry's use of the phrase 'Enigma and Variations' sounds as
though it is the actual title of the work. It is highly improbable that he
would have invented this phrase, and this suggests that Jaeger may
have used this title in some covering letter or possibly in conversation.

There is in fact a certain logic about such a title given that the word
'Enigma' is placed on the score where one might otherwise have
expected the word 'Theme'. So the title 'Enigma and Variations' would
have been equivalent to 'Theme and Variations', a fairly normal name
for a work of this sort.

Jaeger would not have invented it either, which suggests that Elgar
may have been contemplating the use of this title at that time. That
there was some discussion over what to call the work is clear from
Elgar's letter to Jaeger of 28 April (two days before Barry's letter) in
which he says:

> If you really think it wd. be better pray do add Finale to the title – I of
> course should prefer simply
>
> Variations
> Op36
> Edward Elgar[29]

But to return to Barry's 30 April letter. At the end he says:

> I shall be glad of any promptings on the Enigma.

Barry told Elgar that he was in no hurry and Elgar took him at his
word, for when Barry next writes, on 26 May, he has clearly still not
received anything from Elgar:

'I have pretty well got to the end of the horrible Russian things Richter has inflicted upon me, & am ready to start upon your (still more horrible?) Enigmatical Variations...'

It was at some point during the next few days that Elgar sent Barry a letter which formed the basis for the well-known first performance programme note in which Barry quotes Elgar and which I will look at in detail in the next chapter.

The only other reference to the Enigma during this period occurs in one of Elgar's letters to Jaeger (28 May) on a subject unconnected with the *Variations*. Elgar uses the phrase 'another "Enigma"–' introducing a comment concerning the commercial success (or rather lack of it) of *The Black Knight*.[31]

At this point, it is instructive to take a close look at the sequence of events.

21 Feb   Manuscript full score is sent to Vert without the word 'Enigma' over the theme.

9 Mar   Vert writes indicating general approval from Richter, although the conductor has not yet seen the score.

13 Mar   Elgar sends manuscript piano score to Novello. This score has no mention of the word 'Enigma'.

23 Mar   Elgar sends sheet of corrections to Jaeger for incorporation in the orchestral score when this is received back from Richter.

24 Mar   Elgar writes to Ivor Atkins to inform him that Richter has accepted.

8 Apr   Full score arrives in Novello.

10 Apr   First reference to 'Enigma' in Barry's first letter to Elgar.

At some point after the receipt of the full score, Jaeger added the word 'Enigma' above the theme (the handwriting is his). He would clearly not have done this without Elgar's approval and as there is absolutely no reference to the subject in any of the letters between the two men, they must have discussed it during one of Elgar's visits to London.

The only visit Elgar made to London in the period of time outlined above was between 17 and 22 March. He was in London again on 10 April (for a rehearsal of *Caractacus*) but by that time Barry was already writing his first letter. The March visit occurred only days after Jaeger had received the manuscript piano score from Elgar and this would, in fact, have been his first sight of the complete score.

It is only natural, then, that the two men would have discussed the score during Elgar's visit, and indeed we have virtual proof that they did so as in a letter written to Jaeger the day after his return home, Elgar says:

> Here is the sheet of corrections – can you make it out? If not let me know: they are <u>all</u> for the <u>Score</u> – the P F. [= pianoforte, ie, the piano score] is right.[32]

Elgar's use of the definite article – 'the' sheet rather than 'a' sheet – makes it clear that he expected Jaeger to know what sheet he was talking about, having discussed the corrections with him in London. Indeed, it would appear that Elgar expected Jaeger to write the corrections in the score himself, as we can see from his letter of 9 April:

> If you have preserved my list of corrections (& I'll scalp you if you haven't) I will make 'em myself in two minutes – only I <u>should</u> like to see an example of your Scoring.[33]

This being so, that Jaeger should have added the word 'enigma' at the same time as part of the desired corrections sounds plausible.

It would seem likely then that the word 'enigma' as applied to the *Variations* first saw the light of day at some point during Elgar's visit to London between 17 and 22 March 1899. If this is so, the word 'enigma' and the Op 36 *Variations* would have come together five months after the first stirrings of the music itself. Why this should have been so is, I think, a key question and I will return to it in Chapter 3.

Interestingly enough, it also seems likely that the news of Richter's acceptance reached Elgar while he was in London. He didn't know on 13 March, he did by 24 March, and he spent most of the intervening period in London. In fact, we can narrow down the time interval even more, for in his letter to Jaeger the day after his return (23 March) Elgar says:

> Do send a wire & say if the score has arrived – I am getting in a fit lest it shd. miscarry.[34]

Clearly he would not have been expecting the imminent return of the score to Novello if he had not known that Richter had finished with it.

Another important element has survived to help this dating and that is Richter's letter to Vert with which he enclosed the list of works to be performed at his forthcoming concerts. This letter is dated 22 March. At about the same time Richter evidently sent a wire to Vert, as when Elgar tells Dorabella the news a few days later he uses the phrase 'Richter has telegraphed'.

Richter could have sent his wire the day before, for there is a letter dated 22 March written to Elgar by his mother in which she says:

> thanks my dear Edward for the few lines from London – I feel I shall approach you with fear & trembling.[35]

Later on she refers to him as 'my dear hero'. This could well be a reaction to a piece of particularly good news as Richter's acceptance would undoubtedly have been, although it would also have been an expression of maternal pride that her son should have been rehearsing with the Royal Choral Society in preparation for a performance of *Caractacus* in the Albert Hall planned for the following month.

Communication of the news while Elgar was in London, and thus in frequent personal contact with Jaeger, would also explain why there are absolutely no references to it in correspondence between the two men around that time.

From all the foregoing it would appear that Richter's acceptance on the one hand, and the appearance of the Enigma on the other, happened at virtually the same time, and this raises the intriguing question of whether there could conceivably have been any connection between the two events.

Any direct involvement on Richter's part can undoubtedly be excluded, especially as it is clear from his 22 March letter to Vert that he wasn't even sure that his performance of the Variations would be the first:

> Please ask Mr Elgar, whether we shall have the very first performance of his interesting work, or the first a.t.C.? [= at these Concerts][36]

However, it seems more than likely that Richter's acceptance may well have precipitated events on Elgar's side, making necessary some rapid decisions on any outstanding unresolved points as the whole question of the 'Enigma' may have been.

Another intriguing question is how did Barry find out about the 'enigmatical' aspect of the *Variations*, When he first mentioned it in his 10 April letter he did not have a score to hand, as he asks Elgar to send him one. He could possibly either have had a brief glance at the manuscript score with the word 'enigma' added or someone must have told him.

Unless he actually met Elgar during his March visit, it couldn't have been the composer himself as there is no trace of any correspondence between the two men on this subject prior to the 10 April letter.

Barry began that letter as follows:

> I was very glad to hear from Dr. Richter that he will produce a work of yours at one of his forthcoming concerts, & am looking forward to seeing your score, as I am responsible for the programme-notice.[37]

This would seem to confirm that even if they did meet in London, Barry and Elgar did not talk about the *Variations*, as Barry would surely have made reference to such a conversation, and further, he would not have needed to inform Elgar about his programme-writing role.

It also makes clear that it is Richter who has informed Barry about his acceptance of the *Variations*. This obviously suggests the possibility that it was also Richter who mentioned the enigmatical element to him. But how would Richter have known if the word did not appear in the score that Elgar, via Vert, sent to him?

Of course Barry's information could well have come from Jaeger, but his 10 April letter to Elgar seems to indicate that he is unaware of Novello's involvement, as not only are they not mentioned, but Barry asks Elgar to send him the score, thus suggesting that he did not know that Novello had it, which he surely would have known had he talked to Jaeger.

However, despite this, it seems to me that the most likely explanation is that Barry had talked with Jaeger and had been shown the score, albeit briefly.

The birth of the 'Enigma' Variations

Elgar's Op 36 *Variations* were first performed, with the Finale in its original shorter version, on 19 June 1899 in St James' Hall, London, under the direction of Hans Richter. They were played as the final item in the first part of the concert, coming after Dvořák's *Carnaval* Overture, Svendsen's Legend for orchestra *Zorahayda*, and the closing scene from Wagner's *Götterdämmerung*. The second part consisted of an orchestral suite from Rimsky-Korsakov's *The Snow Maiden* and Mozart's *Prague* Symphony.

The work was an immediate success and the first performance marked a major milestone not only in Elgar's career but also in the history of English music as a whole. Apart from one or two grumbles about the concealment of the identities of the subjects of the variations, the critics were unanimous in their praise, and in particular *The Athenaeum* saw the ongoing appeal of the work:

...the Variations will, we feel sure, be often heard, and as often admired.[38]

Elgar received many expressions of congratulations, of which that from Sir Hubert Parry is especially worth quoting, given the 'elder statesman' status which Parry enjoyed at that time:

They [ie, the *Variations*] are indeed a brilliant success, and will bring the old country as well as yourself honour wherever they are heard.[39]

Both *The Athenaeum* and Sir Hubert Parry were spot on in their appraisal as the *Variations* have proved to be one of Elgar's more enduring (and endearing) works. But setting aside these reactions, behind this account of the circumstances of the first performance lies what for me is one of the more intriguing aspects of the birth of the *'Enigma Variations'*: however did Hans Richter get involved?

I can assure the reader that I am not trying to pile puzzle on top of puzzle, creating even more question marks around a work which already has more than its fair share.

Just consider the background.

On the one hand we have the 56-year-old Hungarian-born conductor Richter, who at the time of the first performance was one of the giants on the Western European musical scene. At the age of 23 he was already associated with Richard Wagner and at 33 had conducted the first ever *Ring* cycle at Bayreuth. He had directed the first performances of many works, including Bruckner's Fourth Symphony in 1881 and Brahms's Third in 1883.

At the time of the *Variations* premiere he had just taken over conductorship of the Hallé Orchestra, having previously been in charge of the Vienna Philharmonic Orchestra, a post in which he was succeeded by Gustav Mahler. It is no exaggeration to say that Richter was one of the top three or four international conductors of the time (along with Hans von Bülow, Artur Nikisch and Hermann Levi.)

On the other hand, we have the 41-year-old English composer (at that time almost a contradiction in terms) Elgar, with a limited, although growing, reputation. His biggest purely orchestral work before the *Variations* had been the overture *Froissart*, dating from 1890, which lasts less than fifteen minutes in performance. His choral works, *King Olaf* and *Caractacus* chief among them, were much longer, and although fine works had remained very much in the provincial, often music festival, context. The central London concert halls had heard very little of his music, although *King Olaf* had been given at the Crystal Palace in April 1897 and the *Imperial March* had actually had its first performance there a fortnight later. *Caractacus* was given at the Albert Hall in April 1899 conducted by Elgar himself, and the following month *The Light of Life* was performed by Henry Wood in the Queen's Hall. In the same month the programme for another Queen's Hall concert said that Elgar...

... ranks in the estimation of all competent judges amongst the most able and promising of the younger generation of composers.[40]

But by this time Richter had already accepted the *Variations*.

The contrast between the relative standing of the two men is enormous and on top of this has to be added the fact that when, in January 1899, the first mention of the *Variations* was made to Richter's agent, Vert, who agreed to submit the score to Richter, the work was not even finished in short score, let alone full orchestral score.

So what happened to bring score, Elgar and Richter together on that June day in 1899?

From what we know of Elgar's personality it seems improbable that he would have even dreamed of approaching Richter on his own initiative. It would have taken an enormous dose of brazen cheek to do so, and given his insecurity and self-doubt, I don't think he would have been capable of it.

He certainly wasn't even thinking of a London première, let alone Richter, for another large-scale orchestral work he had in mind at that time. This was the *Gordon* Symphony, which never eventually materialised but which he had hoped to have ready for a first performance at the Worcester Three Choirs Festival in September 1899.

As it turned out, the *Variations* ultimately had a first performance of a kind there, as although it was the third time the work had been played (after London in June and New Brighton in July), it was the first time it was heard in its definitive version with the extended Finale. Other musical projects of that time were also firmly rooted in the provincial music festival context. He was talking with the Norwich organizers in terms of a song cycle, which became *Sea Pictures*, for their festival in October 1899, and he had been asked for a new work for the Birmingham festival of 1900, which eventually materialised in *The Dream of Gerontius*, these two works bearing the opus numbers 37 and 38, immediately following the *Variations*.

Nothing in all this would suggest that it was Elgar who had the idea of a Richter London première for the *Variations*. Indeed, the idea of any London première at all, even with an English conductor such as Henry Wood, must have seemed to him a remote dream. Wood, as it happened, did express interest in producing the *Variations* but by that time (March 1899) the work had already been submitted to Richter.

Whilst on the subject of Henry Wood, various writers have claimed that he actually gave the *Variations* their first rehearsal on 3 June 1899. This idea is purely fanciful, as is clear from Alice's diary entry for that day:

E. to 1st rehearsal of Variations. Richter. St. James' Hall. Much pleased.

Nothing in Elgar's letters around this time suggests a Wood rehearsal, although it is my guess that it was precisely one of his letters which indirectly caused the confusion.

Percy Young, in his collection of Elgar's letters to Jaeger, *Letters to Nimrod*, quotes a letter which begins:

Wood is rehearsing the Vars. at 10.30 tomorrow (Saturday)[41]

At the head of the letter Elgar only wrote the day – Friday – and Dr Young placed it as being 2 June 1899.

In Jerrold Northrop Moore's collection of publishers' letters, he dates this letter as 26 April 1901, and this makes a lot more sense as at that time Wood was preparing for a performance of the work on 4 May. The letter also refers to the 'new arrival' in Jaeger's family, and in fact his second child, a son, had been born earlier that month.[42]

The story of the Wood rehearsal of the *Variations* in June 1899 would seem, then, to derive from Dr Young's original dating of this letter.

But to return to Richter. If it seems improbable that Elgar had the idea of approaching him, Jaeger is another matter. Jaeger was extremely perceptive, and at times proved to be a better judge of Elgar's music than the composer himself. I believe that Jaeger must have realized the quality of Elgar's score and, immersed as he naturally was by his nationality in the great German tradition, thought of Richter as a potential conductor for the first performance.

Jaeger also knew how to bully Elgar into doing things he didn't want to do in a way nobody else could, and thus I can well imagine him nagging away at Elgar to try Richter, and I can equally well imagine Elgar, although outwardly sceptical, being deep within himself attracted by what must have seemed to him a crazy idea.

In fact, Jaeger had hankered after Richter on at least one previous occasion, as we can see from a letter he wrote to Elgar in September 1897 after the first performance of the *Te Deum and Benedictus* in Hereford:

... the Orchestra (...) missed plenty of 'points' of interest a conductor of the stamp of say the great Hans Richter or Mr Henry Wood would have made special features.[43]

It would thus seem rather more likely that the idea of approaching Richter came from Jaeger.

There are two other aspects of this question which seem to me well worth mentioning. The first of these concerns Elgar's reputation at that time, for if it is undoubtedly true that 1899 was a landmark year for him, the momentum had been building up all through 1898.

At the beginning of that year, Elgar reached agreement with the Leeds organizers that he would write a new choral work for their festival in October. This work was *Caractacus*, The festival performance was a triumph, but even before it there had been expressions of interest in performing extracts at the Crystal Palace later that year and the whole work in the Albert Hall the following year. In fact Vert specifically referred to the *Caractacus* success in his letter to Richter accompanying the score.[44]

Hard on the heels of the Leeds success, and very possibly as a result of it, came invitations to write works for Norwich in 1899 and Birmingham in 1900. In fact there had been indications of interest from Birmingham before the first performance of *Caractacus* but it was only in November that it was agreed that Elgar was to have 'the principal place' in the 1900 festival rather than half a programme.

As Jerrold Northrop Moore has said:

The world of the national choral festivals could offer no higher distinction.[45]

This agreement, which came three weeks after the idea of the *Variations* was born, was finalized with Charles Beale of the festival committee, but the Musical Director of the Birmingham Festival at that time was none other than Hans Richter, who had in fact occupied this post since 1885.

Unfortunately, the Birmingham Central Library, although holding a substantial amount of archives relating to the Birmingham Music Festival, has no material covering the year 1898, and so there are no committee meeting minutes to show how Elgar was chosen and to what extent Richter was involved in the choice. However, it would seem reasonable to suppose that Richter was at the very least informed of the choice, for after all it would be his job to give the first performance.

Could it be, then, that the Birmingham commission opened up a connection, albeit indirect, with Richter that Elgar and Jaeger decided to try and use for the *Variations*?

The Norwich commission also has possible connections with the *Variations*. Early in January 1899, Alberto Randegger, the Director of the Norwich festival, wrote to Elgar that they wanted a short work, if possible for contralto, tenor or bass. The contralto retained for the festival was Clara Butt and the story is told of how Elgar went to see her at her London home one day in mid-January (it was in fact Saturday 14 January) but was not received as she was in her bath at the time. He had to return later.

The significance of this connection is that Clara Butt's manager was Vert, who, as we have seen, acted as agent for Richter. Could it be that Elgar, renewing his contacts with Vert, whom he had first met in 1897, decided to try his luck with regard to the *Variations* and Richter?

Elgar clearly recognized a debt of gratitude to Vert, as can be seen from his letter of 13 October 1901:

> I have to thank you for the introduction to Richter which led to the first performance of the work... [46]

Writing to Jaeger in September 1899, Elgar remarked that Vert did the work 'as a favour',[47] and it is certainly true that Vert did go to special lengths to ensure the success of the work, as the same letter tells how he organized at his own expense an extra preliminary rehearsal. As it happened, this extra effort on Vert's part was partially responsible for a temporary rift in relationships between Elgar and Novello due to the fact that, to Elgar's disgust, the latter charged Vert for the hire of the orchestral parts for the extra rehearsal in question. This rift resulted in Elgar's next work, *Sea Pictures*, being entrusted to another publishing house, Boosey & Co.

However, the truth, as is frequently the case, is probably a combination of the circumstances I have described. A series of different factors coming together at a given time to produce a result which at first sight seems surprising.

Before leaving the subject of the birth of the *'Enigma' Variations*, there is another possible influence connected with the first performance which must be mentioned, and that concerns Sir Hubert Parry.

In his biography of Stanford, Harry Plunket Greene, who was Parry's son-in-law, states that Jaeger showed the score of the *Variations* to Parry, who took it enthusiastically to Richter on a rainy night. It has been claimed that this story is impossible, but I would submit that not only is it possible, but there is even a very remote chance that Elgar himself was directly involved.

The first objection to the veracity of the story is that the score which was eventually sent to Richter was not finished until 19 February 1899 and was then sent directly to Vert (ie, without passing through Jaeger's hands). While this is undoubtedly true, it ignores the fact that Elgar developed his music in short score, written, like a piano arrangement, on two staves. It is not impossible that he took this short score with him to show Jaeger when he went to London in January 1899 and therefore Jaeger could have had access to it at that time.

In fact, that January visit, as we have seen, is of vital importance in the history of the *Variations* for it was during it that Vert agreed that Elgar should submit the full score once finished. We can trace Elgar's movements during his stay with some accuracy, largely thanks to Alice's diary:

Mon 9 Jan	Elgar goes to London and sees Randegger re the Norwich Festival. Alice joins Elgar in London by a later train.
Tues 10 Jan	Various visits including tea with Basil Nevinson
Wed 11 Jan	Lunch and evening with Nevinson
Thur 12 Jan	Elgar visits Jaeger alone
Fri 13 Jan	Lunch with his friend Kalisch
Sat 14 Jan	Visits to Clara Butt, Randegger, Nevinson and the Jaegers

Sun 15 Jan	Elgar has a cold. Lunch with Nevinson, Queen's Hall concert in the afternoon and later dinner in honour of the composer Frederic Cowen
Mon 16 Jan	Visit to the London Library
Tues 17 Jan	The Elgars return to Malvern

Three days after returning home, Elgar wrote to Jaeger:

I am not well: ever since I got my head wet – last Thursday – 'along of you'.[48]

The Thursday in question is clearly 12 January, when Elgar visited Jaeger at home. Now unless Jaeger emptied a bucket of water over Elgar, this comment can only mean that Elgar had been out in the rain. Indeed, Meteorological Office records confirm that that day was a particularly unpleasant one and that it was blowing a gale all afternoon and evening.[49]

The phrase 'along of you' is an old-fashioned expression which is presumably why Elgar puts it in inverted commas. It can mean either 'because of you' or 'along with you'. The first definition might suggest that Elgar is complaining that he got his head wet through going to see Jaeger, which sounds somewhat churlish to say the least. However, it could also suggest, as the second definition clearly does, that they were both out in the rain.

What could they have been doing? Going to see Parry perhaps? His home in Kensington Square was not that far from Jaeger's in West Kensington. There is no record of such a visit in any surviving correspondence on either Elgar's or Parry's side, but the combination of Elgar's comment in his letter plus the actual weather conditions that day, plus the Plunket Greene story of Jaeger's visit to Parry on a rainy night, makes the possibility at least plausible.

That bad weather is somehow connected with the *Variations* can also be seen from a letter that Jaeger wrote to Elgar on 7 November 1899 in which the following statement occurs:

> Treacherous weather! Last Sunday in London would have driven you to desperation – or another 'Enigma'.[50]

This may be a reference to the possible visit to Parry on a rainy night, although it may simply be a reflection of the fact that Jaeger knew that Elgar had been feeling in a rather despondent mood on the evening when the Enigma theme first emerged.

Elgar certainly felt a special debt of gratitude to Parry, as can be seen in a letter he wrote to the Editor of *Music and Letters* in 1920:

> The moment to enumerate the many occasions on which Parry advised and encouraged me is not now; I hope to make known all I owe to his ungrudging kindness at some future time.[51]

We know of some instances of Parry's support of Elgar, for example his generous contribution to the cost of Elgar's ceremonial robes for the Honorary Degree in Music at Cambridge University in 1900, or his putting forward of Elgar's name for admission to the Athenaeum in 1904. But the somewhat mysterious tone of Elgar's letter suggests that Parry helped in other ways which for some reason could not be revealed just yet, and indeed, the atmosphere of cliques and intrigues that appears to have existed in musical circles at that time, and which Elgar hated so much, may well have caused him (and possibly also Parry) to consider any approach by this latter to Richter on his behalf as a sensitive issue best treated discreetly. In this context it is relevant to note that at the time of Elgar's letter to *Music and Letters*, although Parry had been dead for two years, Stanford, with whom Elgar had always had strained relations, was still alive.

Before leaving the subject of Parry, it is interesting to note that he has another but quite different connection with the *Variations*, as at an early stage of the development of the work it would seem that Elgar was considering him as a possible 'variant'. However, Elgar was afraid that any such variation would merely be a parody of Parry's style and so the idea was abandoned, as was a possible Sullivan variation for exactly the same reason.

Notes

1. Maine – p 101

2. Article signed 'Musicus'. Newspaper held in Sheffield Central Library

3. Moore – *Publishers' Letters* – p 95

4. Ibid – p 92

5. Note in the Elgar Birthplace quoted in Anderson – p 91

6. Burley/Carruthers – p 116

7. Powell – p 12

8. Burley/Carruthers – p 116

9. Powell – p 12

10. Burley/Carruthers – p 117

11. Moore – *Publishers' Letters* – p 96

12. Ibid – p 102

13. Moore – Lifetime Letters – p 73

14. Moore – *Publishers' Letters* – p 115

15. Ibid – p 108

16. Ibid – p 74

17. Reproduced in Atkins opposite p 195

18. Moore – *Publishers' Letters* – p 300

19. Ibid – p 407

20. Ibid – p 89

21. Ibid – p 315

22. Ibid – p 243

23. Ibid – p 111

24. Powell – p 14

25. Atkins – p 42

26. Powell – p 15

27. HWRO 705:445:3034

28. HWRO 705:445:3038

29. Moore – *Publishers' Letters* – p 121

30. HWRO 705:445:3035

31. Moore – *Publishers' Letters* – p 124

32. Ibid – p 116

33. Ibid – p 119

34. Ibid – p 116

35. Moore – *Lifetime Letters* – p 76

36. Reproduced in Redwood opposite p 97

37. HWRO 705:445:3034

38. Young – *Friends Pictured Within* – p 83 : published in Monk (ed) – *Elgar Studies*

39. Moore – *Lifetime Letters* – p 32

40. Wood – p 125

41. Young – *Nimrod Letters* – p 51

42. Moore – *Publishers' Letters* – p 286

43. Ibid – p 50

44. Quoted in the introduction of the Elgar Complete Edition of the *Variations*

45. Moore – *Life* – p 256

46. Moore – *Publishers' Letters* – p 302

47. Ibid – p 136

48. Ibid – p 102

49. Letter to author from National Meteorological Library & Archive, Bracknell, 21 Nov 1995

50. Moore – *Publishers' Letters* – p 148

51. Moore – *Lifetime Letters* – p 332

2 – The Enigma

The nature of the Enigma

Despite the fact that the Op 36 *Variations* are now referred to universally as the *'Enigma' Variations* and indeed have been for many years – in the Elgar Birthplace in Broadheath there is an unidentified newspaper cutting dated 19 October 1901 which talks of '... Dr. Elgar's *'Enigma' Variations'* – this was not Elgar's title for the work.

The title he adopted is quite simply *Variations*. As we saw in the last chapter, Jaeger at one stage suggested adding the word 'Finale', presumably to give 'Variations and Finale' but Elgar did not like the idea. It will be recalled that his preference was quite clear:

> ... I of course should prefer simply
>
> Variations
> Op36
> Edward Elgar[1]

Which is what he got. He again referred to the simplicity of the title in another letter to Jaeger in November 1899 concerning proofs for the printed full score in which he suggested a form of type...

> ... not <u>too</u> far removed from the austerity of the title.[2]

There is an important point here which is worth stressing. Elgar did *not* call his Op 36 'Variations on an Original Theme' which is the 'official' title it has invariably been given ever since (and indeed this is how the title is given in the 1986 Elgar Complete Edition of the score). The manuscript full score which was sent to Vert has 'Variations for Orchestra', as does the manuscript piano score sent to Jaeger in March 1899, and this would indicate that the reference to an original theme had already been dropped before the addition of the word 'enigma'.

This is odd. Composers of variations generally specify what their variations are based on, along the lines of 'Variations on a Theme of so-and-so', or 'Variations on an Original Theme', or even simply 'Theme and Variations'. In two of his letters written during the composition of the *Variations*, Elgar referred to an original theme; thus, for example, in October 1898 to Jaeger:

... I have sketched a set of Variations (orkestra) on an original theme[3]

And in February 1899 to FG Edwards:

Just completed a set of Symphonic Variations (theme original) for orchestra ...[4]

But he never again used the term 'original theme' when referring to the *Variations*, at least as far as we can tell from the surviving records.

He did introduce the word 'enigma' but not, however, in the title of the work. The word appears over the theme at the very start of the work, and it is clear from the way it was added at a late stage to the manuscript full score, where it appears just alongside the metronome marking for the theme, that the word applies only to the theme and not to the whole work.

Confirmation of this can be found in a letter to Jaeger in June 1899 in which Elgar, talking of the Finale, refers to

... the principal motive (Enigma)...[5]

Further confirmation can be found in Elgar's notes on *The Music Makers* in 1912:

I have used the opening bars of the theme (Enigma) of the Variations...[6]

So, bearing in mind that the 'enigma' is the theme, what is it all about?

CA Barry's programme note for the first performance on 19 June 1899, based on information received from Elgar himself, is an important and frequently quoted document. Its importance is such that I make no apology for quoting it yet again:

45

The Enigma I will not explain – its 'dark saying' must be left unguessed, and I warn you that the apparent connexion between the Variations and the Theme is often of the slightest texture; further, through and over the whole set another and larger theme 'goes' but is not played ... So the principal Theme never appears, even as in some late dramas – e.g., Maeterlinck's 'L'Intruse' and 'Les Sept Princesses'– the chief character is never on the stage.[7]

It would appear that this statement has two aspects:

1) The 'Enigma', what it represents and its relation to the rest of the work.
2) The 'larger' theme which 'goes' but is not played.

The first of these two points, where Elgar is clearly referring to the theme, is easily explained and the supporting evidence is solid.

For a start, Elgar's seemingly cryptic comment about the 'dark saying' which must be left unguessed is a direct reference to definitions of the word 'enigma' with which he must have been familiar.

As Geoffrey Hodgkins pointed out some years ago, Webster's Dictionary, quoting Johnson, gave:

A dark saying, in which some known thing is concealed under obscure language; an obscure question; a riddle. A question, saying or painting, containing a hidden meaning, which is proposed to be guessed.[8]

Similarly, Dr Percy Young points out that 'dark saying' is the translation of the Greek 'αἴνιγμα' (ainigma), given in the edition of Liddell and Scott's (abridged) Lexicon current at the time.[9]

Elgar's use of the phrases 'dark saying' (which he puts in inverted commas thus indicating a quotation) and 'unguessed' (strange word in any other context), are surely direct references to the dictionary definition. Any other conclusion implies an incredible coincidence. 'Unguessed' also recalls C A Barry's references to 'guessing' the enigma in his letters quoted in the last chapter. It should not be forgotten that the famous programme note was quoted by Barry from a letter Elgar wrote to him in response to these letters.

What Elgar is therefore saying here, in a deliberately erudite reference (he was given to this sort of thing, see the reference to Maeterlinck in almost the next breath), is quite simply that he will not disclose what the Enigma (ie, the theme) represents. In view of this, Professor Ian Parrott's convoluted although admittedly ingenious excursions into the Bible and in particular St Paul's phrase in the first letter to the Corinthians – 'for now we see through a glass, darkly' - are obviously way off the mark.

But despite Elgar's unwillingness to give explanations on this topic, we have sufficient evidence to assert that the 'Enigma' theme represents Elgar himself. The clearest evidence is his use of the first phrase of the theme as a kind of musical signature on two occasions in letters to Dorabella.

The first of these, dated 10 October 1901, leaves no doubt that Elgar means this phrase to be associated with himself as he uses it in place of a signature after using three phrases from Dorabella's variation in his letter, the first of which replaces her name in the opening 'Dear...'.[10]

The second, written a fortnight later, uses these musical phrases in exactly the same sort of way:

It is so long since I saw you that I forget if you really are nice or if somebody only imagined you to be. So you must come and tell us... whether you are as nice as... (first phrase of Dorabella variation)... or only as unideal as... (first phrase of 'Enigma' theme). [11]

Phrases from other variations were also used in correspondence to their respective subjects, for instance, Jaeger (Elgar's letter of 27 June 1900)[12] and Troyte Griffith (25 November 1898)[13].

In the first of the letters to Dorabella referred to above, Elgar wrote the word 'mesto' above the phrase from the 'Enigma' theme. The *Concise Grove's* definition of this Italian term is 'sad, sorrowful, dejected'. These sentiments echo the 'desolate streams' of *The Music Makers* and it was at the occurrence of these words that Elgar re-used the 'Enigma' theme in that work:

I have used the opening bars of the theme (Enigma) of the Variations because it expressed when written (in 1898) my sense of the loneliness of the artist...[14]

The term 'mesto' does actually appear in the score of the theme, although there it is written above the first violin part in the penultimate bar and not over the phrase quoted in the letter to Dorabella.

The 'Enigma' theme, then, represents Elgar himself, or, more accurately, his frame of mind when he wrote it.

As far as the 'connexion' between the theme and the variations is concerned, despite Elgar's statement there is a very obvious relationship in all cases except two, but I will return to this point in Chapter 4.

Before leaving the subject of the identification of the 'Enigma' theme with Elgar himself, I should mention the observation made by Michael Kennedy to the effect that the name 'Edward Elgar' goes in almost natural speech rhythm with the first phrase of the theme.[15]

This is undoubtedly true but cannot, I think, be advanced in support of the identification of Elgar himself with the theme, as the same can be said for many other names: Alice Elgar, Dora Penny (and even Dorabella) and Mary Lygon among the variations; Hubert Leicester, Ivor Atkins, Rosa Burley and Helen Weaver among past and present acquaintances of Elgar who were not variations. The point is that literally millions of names 'go' with these first four notes (including, as it happens, my own).

Michael Kennedy's observation is, then, interesting but basically for its curiosity value rather than as a serious argument.

The larger theme that 'goes'

The 'larger theme that "goes" but is not played' is the aspect of the Op 36 *Variations* which has most fired imaginations since the first performance a century ago. This phrase has been dissected and analysed many times since then with three words in particular the object of interest: 'larger', 'theme' and 'goes'.

Of these, 'theme' has perhaps provoked most speculation and has given rise to two schools of thought. The first claims that 'theme' is used in a musical sense (ie, melody, tune), whilst the second favours an abstract interpretation of the word (ie, concept, idea).

The weight of the available evidence is overwhelmingly in favour of the musical sense.

For a start, the context of the programme note already makes the sense clear. The phrase 'another and larger theme' occurs in the same sentence as the phrase 'the Variations and the Theme', which is clearly referring to the musical theme of the 'Enigma'. In addition, we are told that 'the larger theme "goes" but is not played'. Only a musical theme can be played.

Elgar's habitual use of the word 'theme' is also instructive. For instance, in a letter he wrote to Jaeger 11 days after the first performance of the *Variations* he says, referring to the Finale:

I <u>could</u> go on with those themes for ½ a day ...[16]

On another occasion he wrote in Ivor Atkins' vocal score of *The Kingdom*:

some themes go with my friends ...[17]

... followed by a musical quotation he associated with Atkins.

Examples such as these abound, but I have been unable to find one single instance of Elgar using the word 'theme' in a non-musical sense.

All those who were close to Elgar at the time of writing the *Variations* believed that the hidden theme was a tune of some sort. Thus Dorabella:

Elgar made it perfectly clear to us(...) that the Enigma was concerned with a tune.[18]

And his daughter Carice:

We know that there was a tune.[19]

And Winifred Norbury:

I always consider that I know the hidden tune in the Enigma ...[20]

Even Troyte tried to guess, but Troyte also had another experience which is even more tantalising:

One Sunday when I went into the study at Craeglea [*sic*], the piano was open and stuck on the notes bits of stamp edge with numbers written on them. 'What's this for?' I asked. That's for you', said Elgar. 'Learn the numbers by heart and observe carefully that some of the notes have more than one number. When you can remember them hit the notes in order with one finger hard and fast.' After a few shots I got it right. That's it', said Elgar, 'Hit 'em harder and keep your finger stiff.' I said, 'I believe it's a tune. What is it?' Elgar laughed and said, 'Oh nothing, we only wanted to hear what it sounded like when you played it.' That tune must have been the theme.[21]

We actually have confirmation of this story from Elgar's side.[22] Both versions agree in all essential details and both link the episode with the hidden theme. Both versions also state that the episode happened in Craeg Lea, one of the houses Elgar lived in in Malvern, into which he moved in March 1899, a month after the *Variations* were completed in full score.

All of the foregoing argues in favour of a musical theme. Two other pieces of evidence argue in the same direction and in addition throw important light on the meaning of the word 'goes'.

In October 1900, coinciding with the first performance of *The Dream of Gerontius*, Elgar was the subject of a biographical article in the *Musical Times* written by its editor, F G Edwards. This article contains a paragraph referring to the *Variations* which is of vital importance, although surprisingly it has not been frequently quoted in the various writings on the subject.

The paragraph reads thus:

In connection with these much discussed Variations, Mr. Elgar tells us that the heading 'Enigma' is justified by the fact that it is possible to add another phrase, which is quite familiar, above the original theme that he has written. What that theme is no one knows except the composer. Thereby hangs the Enigma.[23]

Prior to publication of this article, Edwards went to great pains to get his facts right. He spent time with Elgar in Malvern in early September 1900, and subsequently submitted drafts of his article to him for comment and correction. Both Elgar and his wife asked for changes to be made and a comparison of the Elgars' requests and the final article shows that virtually all of their requests were complied with.[24]

Elgar was therefore fully aware of, and presumably happy with, the paragraph concerning the *Variations* as he did not ask for any modification. In this paragraph the hidden theme is referred to as a phrase. Now although the word 'phrase' has a literary meaning in the sense of a series of words, it can by no means be interpreted as a concept or an abstract idea.

The first-ever biography of Elgar was published in 1904 by R J Buckley, the music critic of *The Birmingham News*. Buckley had known Elgar for a long time and had first visited him at home in 1896. So the two men had known each other personally for some years prior to the publication of the biography, and there must have been mutual trust as Elgar agreed to collaborate with Buckley during the writing of the book.

Buckley, in fact, adopted the same approach as Edwards had done for his *Musical Times* article four years earlier, and visited Elgar in March 1904 to discuss the project and then sent him proofs for comment before finalizing the text for publication.

The published text can therefore be considered to have Elgar's blessing, and indeed in his introduction Buckley has the confidence to say:

Whatever this book states as fact may be accepted as such.[25]

In it, and with reference to the *Variations*, occurs the following statement:

the theme is a counterpoint on some well-known melody which is never heard.[26]

This confirms that the hidden theme is a melody and does so in terms which do not permit any misunderstanding whatsoever.

Many writers on this subject have stated that at no time is Elgar known to have said that the hidden theme was a tune. Whilst strictly speaking true, the fact that both Edwards and Buckley are clearly referring to tunes in texts which were submitted to Elgar for approval surely makes the matter clear beyond reasonable doubt. For in the final analysis it has to be recognized that all these early statements concerning a hidden theme, no matter who made them, ultimately derive from Elgar himself.

And alongside all this has to be put the fact that there is not one single shred of evidence to support the idea of the hidden theme as an abstract concept. It is a notion which seems to have been born out of a sort of frustration that no hidden musical theme has ever been satisfactorily identified.

Nevertheless, there is no escaping the fact that if we are to draw conclusions firmly based on the available evidence, then the hidden theme is a tune which 'goes' in counterpoint with the 'Enigma' theme.

The extent of the counterpoint

At this point, I should mention two objections which have been raised concerning the existence of a hidden theme.

The first of these stems directly from the precise wording of Barry's programme note:

through and over the whole set another and larger theme goes...

It has been plausibly argued that it is impossible to find a theme which 'goes', as if in counterpoint, for example, with every variation. I will return to this point later.

The second objection was pointed out by Percy Young and concerns an early sketch for the *Variations* in which it would seem that Elgar at one stage contemplated the middle section of the theme in eight bars instead of the four of the final version. As Dr Young says:

> ... the earliest existing sketch puts difficulties in the way. The middle section was originally planned as an 8-bar phrase and its reduction to 4 bars leaves any suppositious counter-theme adrift.[27]

However, I would suggest that there is sufficient evidence to show that the 'Enigma' theme is that stated in the first six bars of the music (ie, not including the middle section), and that therefore the hidden theme must 'go' in counterpoint with those six bars.

The most striking evidence, it seems to me, is the double bar at the end of the first six bars. Double bars are used to mark off different sections of a piece and Elgar uses them more than once in the *Variations*, for example:

– after the first two bars of the first variation (C.A.E.), which really only serve as a connecting passage, the real beginning of the variation coming after the double bar;

– a very similar situation after the first two bars of Variation XII (B.G.N.);

– three times in the Finale, each time at the beginning of a new 'section';

– once in Variation X in the same sort of way.

Clearly Elgar wished to mark a separation between the main theme of the 'Enigma' and the four bars of the middle section in G major. It seems to me highly unlikely that he would have done this if the two sections had been intimately interconnected by the presence of a hidden theme going with both. This, in turn, would suggest that the hidden theme goes in counterpoint with the first six bars only.

Furthermore, as we have already seen, the music of those first six bars had a special significance for Elgar as is evidenced by his use of the first phrase as a musical signature in letters to Dorabella, and the re-use of almost the whole six bars in *The Music Makers*.

Additional evidence can be derived from Elgar's letter to Jaeger of 30 June 1899 in which Elgar, talking about the Finale, says:

– the principal motive (Enigma) comes in grandioso...[28]

This occurs at Figure 68 in the score when the theme appears in its 'Nimrod' guise in the major. The music of the middle section is nowhere in evidence in this part of the Finale, thus leaving no doubt as to which thematic material Elgar had in mind when he used the word 'Enigma'.

So from everything that we have seen so far in this chapter, it can be concluded that on the basis of the available evidence, there is a hidden theme, and that this hidden theme is a musical one with which the first six bars of the *Variations* theme 'go' in counterpoint.

However, before continuing, there is another possibility which must be looked at. Given that, as I have observed, all the earliest statements we have concerning the hidden theme ultimately derive from Elgar himself, there is the possibility that for some reason he made the whole thing up and that the hidden theme is pure fiction.

The possibility of a hoax

It has more than once been suggested that there never was any hidden theme and that the whole rigmarole surrounding the enigma is nothing more than a hoax.

Billy Reed of the London Symphony Orchestra, and a close friend of Elgar's from around 1909 until his death, quotes Jaeger as saying that it was...

... a bit of Elgar's humour.[29]

Unfortunately, Reed gives no details as to when Jaeger said this or to whom. But the idea expressed finds an echo in Percy Young:

... the best 'jape' [a word much used by Elgar] of all is the absence of any enigma...[30]

Apart from Elgar's well-known love of puzzles of all kinds, no evidence has ever been adduced to support this suggestion, although again, it may simply be a reaction to the fact that the enigma has never been satisfactorily solved. But nonetheless the suggestion has been made and must therefore be considered.

The first thing to be said is that although it is indisputably true that Elgar was very partial to 'japes' of all kinds, only on very few occasions did this spill over into his music. He never wrote, for example, a Divertimento or any sort of deliberately humorous or 'jokey' music. There are lighthearted moments in his music – the Salvation Army band in *Cockaigne*, for instance, or even Falstaff getting happily drunk in *Falstaff* – but these examples are firmly rooted in the context of the music and therefore their prime objective is not amusement for its own sake.

He enjoyed 'erudite' jokes, for example the fact that the first *Pomp and Circumstance March*, which is written in D, in fact starts off a semi-tone higher in E flat.

There are also deliberate mystifications of a non-musical kind, of which the best-known is undoubtedly the quotation in Spanish at the head of the Violin Concerto...

Aquí está encerrada el alma de.....
(Herein is enshrined the soul of.....)

There is also the mysterious apparent place-name 'Leyrisch Turasp' at the end of the Op 60 songs.

But these examples are rare and there is no known case of Elgar creating a hoax connected with any of his works. Which doesn't necessarily mean, of course, that he never did it, but the available evidence makes it unlikely.

But to me a much stronger argument is provided by possible motivation. Why would Elgar have invented a hidden theme which didn't exist?

We have already seen that the enigma was totally absent from the period covering the composition and scoring of the *Variations*. The score was sent to Richter via his agent on 21 February 1899 and it was almost exactly a month later that the news of approval came back. So Elgar knew that the great man would conduct the first performance of the *Variations* before any mention is made anywhere of the enigma.

So why invent a hoax? The music certainly didn't need it to succeed, as Elgar must have known and has been so convincingly demonstrated since. Indeed, the idea of an enigma might even have produced a negative reaction, as was the case with the hidden identities of the 'friends pictured within'. The *Musical News* review of the first performance said of the *Variations*...

> That they are severally labelled with the initials of certain friends of the composer (...) we hold to be a mistake.[31]

Clearly, it cannot be conclusively proved that the enigma was not a hoax, but all the evidence we have, combined with a measure of logical reasoning and common sense, suggests very strongly that it wasn't.

Notes

1. Moore – *Publishers' Letters* – p 121

2. Ibid – p 153

3. Ibid – p 95

4. Ibid – p 108

5. Ibid – p 128

6. Introductory note to *The Music Makers* sent to Ernest Newman, who was to write the first performance programme note. Quoted in Moore – *Lifetime Letters* – p 249

7. First performance programme notes by C A Barry

8. ESJ – Sept 1979 – p 30

9. Young – *Friends Pictured Within* – p 104 (fn 5): published in Monk (ed) – *Elgar Studies*

10. reproduced in Powell between pp 38 and 39

11. Ibid – p38

12. Moore – *Publishers' Letters* – p 206

13. reproduced in Young – Elgar Letters opposite 104

14. see note 6

15. Kennedy – *Portrait* – p 86

16. Moore – *Publishers' Letters* – p 128

17. reproduced in Atkins opposite p 154

18. Powell – p 119

19. quoted in Powell – p 120

20. quoted in Powell – p 120

21. Young – *Friends Pictured Within* – p 102: published in Monk (ed) – *Elgar Studies*

22. Atkins – p 428

23. Redwood – p 47

24. Moore – *Publishers' Letters* – pp 235 – 240

25. Buckley – Introduction

26. Ibid – p 54

27. Young – *Elgar O M* – p 279

28. Moore – *Publishers' Letters* – p 128

29. Reed – *Elgar* – p 53

30. Young – *Elgar O M* – p 279

31. *Musical News* – 24 June 1899

3 – Hypotheses

Thus far we have looked at the birth of the *Variations* and the Enigma, and the nature of this latter and to what it refers.

Now it is necessary to try and make sense of all this, pulling together all the different strands into some sort of coherence. In order to do this, I would like to propose a series of hypotheses, which, I hasten to add, are firmly based on all the evidence. Nevertheless, in order to keep quite separate fact and hypothesis, I will specify what is which, adding details of the logic behind the reasoning in each case.

Where the hidden theme came from

Fact: Elgar came home one October evening after a violin teaching session at Rosa Burley's school 'The Mount'. After dinner he sat down at the piano and started to play. At some point he played a tune which his wife noticed and asked him to repeat, and which he later indicated was a counterpoint on a well-known theme.

Hypothesis: That theme was one he had heard the same day in Rosa Burley's school.

Rationale: It seems reasonable to suppose that the theme was one which was fresh in Elgar's memory or which was stuck in his head as a result of a recent stimulus. We all have tunes which stick in our head from time to time and Elgar was no exception, as can be seen from a letter he wrote to Jaeger in June 1898:

> I have Taylors [*sic*] theme jigging in the vacuities of my head [1]

That Elgar had heard or been reminded of the theme at 'The Mount' seems, therefore, a perfectly plausible possibility.

Comment: The significance of it is that it would throw light on a comment later made by Rosa Burley which has up until now defied all rational explanation. That comment was:

I'm not a variation; I'm the theme.[2]

If one imagines Elgar later mentioning to Rosa Burley that his inspiration derived from a tune he had heard that October day in her school, without necessarily identifying the tune, then her seemingly eccentric claim suddenly makes some sense, for she would indeed have been associated with the theme, albeit the hidden one.

I should perhaps add that this hypothesis has another significance which will become clear when we look at solutions to the 'enigma' in Chapter 6.

From hidden theme to variations

Fact: Having repeated his tune for his wife, Elgar said that it was nothing but something might be made of it, and then played a version as one of the *Variations'* subjects might have done (as we have already seen, there are conflicting versions of which one.)

Hypothesis: Elgar told his wife that his tune was a counterpoint on the other theme, and explained that that was how he felt it in his current state of mind. Anybody else doing what he was doing would have felt it differently.

Rationale: If we accept all Elgar's later statements about the hidden theme, then it seems to me inconceivable that on that October evening, when neither *Variations* nor Enigma yet existed, he would not have mentioned it to his wife. Why would he have hidden it?

Furthermore, there is something odd about Elgar's quoted version of events. We read that when his wife asked him what was the tune he had played, he replied:

> nothing – but something might be made of it; Powell would have done this...[3]

When a composer imagines a theme, his first thoughts are surely not what someone else would do with it. However, if Elgar explained to his wife that his tune was his particular version of another theme, then the following comment 'Powell would have done this', referring to what Powell would have done had he been doing what Elgar was doing, ie, playing a version of the other theme to suit his frame of mind, makes absolute sense.

Comments:As we have just seen, this hypothesis makes sense of Elgar's account of how he proceeded from his tune to the variations.

But it also makes sense of more. The mechanism, it seems to me, was the following: Elgar created his version, later said to be a counterpoint of the hidden theme. He then created a series of ideas as to how other people would have interpreted the hidden theme, but using his version as a base.

Therefore all his variations are related to the hidden theme. They are, in essence, variations once removed. For if a theme can be schematized as, say, A-B-C, then a variation would be A1-B1-C1. A variation on this latter might be B1-A1-C1, but the underlying A-B-C is still there.

If I am insisting on this point, it is because I believe that this is the significance of the phrase in Barry's programme note, certainly quoted from Elgar, to the effect that...

> through and over the whole set another and larger theme 'goes', but is not played...

In effect, Elgar's Op 36 is a set of variations on a variation on a theme, and one wonders whether this was not what Alice Elgar might have meant when she reportedly said to her husband...

you are doing something which I think has never been done before.[4]

The reason behind the Enigma

Fact: In the early days of writing the *Variations*, Elgar spoke of an 'original theme'. This denomination then disappears from the surviving records, whilst the word 'enigma' appears after completion of the score but before the first performance.

Hypothesis: In January 1899 Elgar discussed the *Variations* with Jaeger and during this discussion one of two things happened. Either Elgar explained to Jaeger the fact that the *Variations* theme was a counterpoint on another theme or, just possibly, Jaeger might have spotted it himself. Either way, the ever-sensible Jaeger pointed out the potential for serious embarrassment if someone else spotted the counterpoint concerning what Elgar was claiming to be an original theme.

But for some reason, probably because the hidden theme was a 'popular' one which, if identified with the *Variations*, might also be embarrassing, neither man thought it wise to identify the hidden theme.

They decided on a clever compromise. Elgar would stop referring to his theme as an 'original' theme and the work would be called simply *Variations*, whilst a way would be sought of identifying the theme itself in such a way as to be able to acknowledge that there was a hidden theme behind it, without revealing the identity of that theme.

Rationale: By mid-March 1899, Elgar already knew that Hans Richter was willing to conduct the first performance of his *Variations*. He must have been delighted, jubilant even, and so why rock the boat?

And yet the word 'enigma' enters into the story. Why?

Taking into consideration all the arguments put forward so far in this study, including the conclusion that there was no hoax, I can think of no other explanation than that offered by this hypothesis.

It is certainly demonstrable that Elgar was actually expecting someone to find the hidden theme, hence his teasing of Dorabella which prompted her to remark in her book...

he egged me on to go on thinking till I got it, and I really believe he would have been pleased and amused if I had done so.[5]

As late as 1923 Elgar commented to Troyte...

... it is so well-known that it is extraordinary that no one has spotted it [6]

As far as the popular nature of the hidden theme is concerned, this can be deduced from the unwillingness to reveal its identity. Had the hidden theme been by Beethoven, for instance, then acknowledging that fact would even have added something to the credentials of Elgar's enigma theme. If he had to acknowledge that there was a hidden theme, then no possible harm could have been done by identifying its impeccable pedigree. Quite the contrary.

But a 'popular' theme would have had precisely the opposite effect. A H Fox Strangways, writing in 1935 on the possibility of *Auld Lang Syne* being the hidden theme, cited one objection to this as...

that a tune so trite or with such superficial or perfunctory associations is unworthy of Elgar's work.[7]

Elgar in 1899, still struggling to make his name nationally and suspicious of the English musical establishment, would surely have been acutely aware of the embarrassing implications of identifying a popular tune as the hidden theme.

Comments: I am therefore suggesting that the adoption of the word 'Enigma', far from being a deliberate and calculated puzzle on Elgar's part, was very much an afterthought. In effect it was a sort of insurance policy, to avoid any possible embarrassment or whatever should anyone have spotted the hidden theme.

It also neatly explains why, as the years went by and the hidden theme remained undiscovered, Elgar was more and more reluctant even to talk about it, let alone reveal its identity. As we have seen, in the early days he was clearly expecting someone to come up with the answer, but as it became increasingly apparent that the secret seemed safe, so he became more defensive with respect to it.

And yet some people knew. It is more or less generally accepted that both Alice and Jaeger knew and this would be confirmed if my hypotheses are correct. But who else?

Dorabella, very close to Elgar at the time, didn't know, although it would seem that Elgar thought that she was the most likely person to arrive at the answer:

I thought that you of all people would guess it.[8]

She certainly attempted a number of solutions and at one point even tried to sweet-talk Jaeger into letting her into the secret. He resisted by appealing to her sense of loyalty to Elgar:

Now, Dorabella, you must be a good girl and not ask me about that. I do not suppose that I could keep it from you if you were to plead with me, but the dear E.E. did make me promise not to tell you.[9]

Neither Troyte nor Billy Reed managed to find out and both were close to Elgar at different times. I don't think Ivor Atkins knew as he would surely have hinted something to his son, Wulstan, at some point, in the same way that the story of Elgar's fiancée, Helen Weaver, was transmitted, albeit with an instruction to wait for 50 years after Elgar's death before revealing it.

I have no evidence to suggest that anyone else was in the secret, although I would hazard a guess that Elgar's daughter Carice knew. She was only eight when the *Variations* were first performed but it is difficult to believe that she didn't ask her father at some later stage. And how would the father refuse to trust his daughter? It is true that Carice wrote in 1969:

I fear we shall none of us ever know for certain.[10]

But she also wrote in 1942:

We know that there was a tune...[11]

My guess is that, as on other aspects other famous father's life, she knew how to be discreetly evasive.

Notes

1. Moore – *Publishers' Letters* – p 78

2. Kennedy – *Portrait* – p 96

3. Maine – p 101

4. Ibid

5. Powell – p 23

6. quoted in Powell – p 119

7. *Music & Letters* – Jan 1935, reprinted in Redwood – p 56

8. quoted in Powell – p 119

9. Ibid – p 28

10. quoted in Parrott – p 49

11. quoted in Powell – p 120

4 – Questions of Identity in the Variations

The identification of the variations

If the circumstances surrounding the 'Enigma' have remained obscure for a century, at least the identity of the 'friends pictured within' has long ceased to provoke speculation, at least, all but one. But, first things first.

Elgar apparently thought that the idea of 'picturing friends within' was a new one:

> I have, in the Variations, sketched 'portraits' of my friends – a new idea I think – that is in each Variation I have 'looked at' the theme through the personality (as it were) of another Johnny... [1]

According to Maine's account of the events of the evening the *Variations* were born, Alice Elgar also thought that the idea was new:

> You are doing something which I think has never been done before.[2]

In fact, as various writers have pointed out, the idea was not new as not only had Schumann done something similar, but there had actually been an earlier *'Enigma' Variations*, a solo piano piece by the English composer Cipriani Potter written in the style of five eminent artists. Although virtually unknown today, Potter was a highly esteemed and prolific composer and his output includes nine symphonies, three piano concertos and a variety of chamber works. He was the first-ever piano professor at the newly founded Royal Academy of Music in 1822 and went on to occupy the post of Principal from 1832 to 1859. It has even been said of him that his music marks the real beginning of the renaissance of English music in general, a process which was to fully flower in the music of Elgar himself.

Potter's prominence in the first half of the last century – he died in 1871 – was such that Elgar must have known of him, although it seems to me highly unlikely that he was aware of the earlier *'Enigma' Variations*. Had he been so, in view of his extreme sensitivity to any suggestion of 'echoes' of other people's work in his own, he would undoubtedly never have dreamed of using the word 'enigma' in connection with his own work, although, as we have seen, he never used the word in the title of his work and it was not in his mind when the work was conceived.

But to return to the identification of the variations, Elgar really didn't seek to hide the identity of his 'variants' as Dorabella called them. With one exception (Variation XIII), all the variations were identified with initials or names. The most transparent of these is Variation VII, 'Troyte', where part of Arthur Troyte Griffith's surname serves as title. Eight of the variations are headed with the initials of the subjects portrayed. One, Variation VI, has a slightly modified form of the subject's christian name – 'Ysobel' for Isabel Fitton. One, Variation X, is Elgar's affectionate nickname for the subject – 'Dorabella' for Dora Penny. One, the Finale, headed 'E.D.U.', referring to Elgar himself, uses his wife's term of endearment for him – Edu (or Edoo as it appears in Alice's diaries) – short for 'Eduard', the German version of Elgar's christian name.

All of these would have been readily recognizable to anybody who knew the 'variant' in question or who had some contact with Elgar, his family, and his circle of friends.

The remaining two, Variations IX and XIII, are the only ones whose title is not a direct reference to the 'variant's' name.

Variation IX, titled 'Nimrod', portrays Jaeger. I can trace no direct evidence that Elgar used 'Nimrod' as a nickname for Jaeger before the *Variations*. Indeed, in his letters it was only less than two months before the birth of the *Variations* that Elgar stopped addressing Jaeger as

'Dear Mr Jaeger', dropping the 'Mr' in favour of the less formal 'Dear Jaeger'.

However, long before this change of style, the letters had become delightfully informal, at times almost intimate. It is not impossible, therefore, that Elgar had already used 'Nimrod' when talking to Jaeger before the *Variations*.

Arguing against this is Elgar's letter of 24 October 1898 to Jaeger, the first to mention the *Variations*, in which he says:

I've labelled 'em with the nicknames of my particular friends - you are Nimrod.[3]

Now one would have supposed that if the nickname had already been used by Elgar then Jaeger would have known that he was 'Nimrod', whereas this rather sounds as if Elgar is telling Jaeger of his nickname for the first time.

It should also be noted that, despite Elgar's statement, only two of the variations are labelled with nicknames (three if one includes E.D.U.) Dorabella's nickname predated the *Variations,* albeit only by a month or so. But it existed, and it was also a simple extension of Dora Penny's christian name (although with echoes of *Così fan Tutte*).

So why was Jaeger's variation the only one of the whole set to have a name specially invented for it? Why not A.J.J.? (Interestingly enough, the dedication of Dorabella's book, *Memories of a Variation*, is: 'To the memory of A.J.J.' whereas one would have expected, given the title of her book and the intense pride which she obviously felt at 'being' a variation: 'To the memory of Nimrod').

The only answer I can suggest is that Elgar felt very close to Jaeger, and indeed owed him a lot, felt supported by him, understood by him. I suggest, then, that the use of the nickname indicates a very special sort of affection, going a long way beyond the sort of friendship Elgar had with the rest of the 'variants'. The music itself is surely indicative of this.

This reasoning would also explain the use of Dorabella's nickname, for whilst his relationship with her was different from that with Jaeger,

Elgar at that particular time was undoubtedly very fond of her, as his letters to her show. It seems to me that there is no doubt that of all the 'friends pictured within', Jaeger and Dorabella were in their different ways closest to Elgar at the time of the *Variations*.

But if this line of argument is sound, then it gives rise to another question. Why 'only' C.A.E. for his wife? He used her affectionate name for him in E.D.U., did he not have an affectionate name for her? These questions open up the whole complex subject of Elgar's relationship with his wife which goes well beyond the scope of the present study. Suffice it to say that the terms of endearment that existed were probably considered too intimate to use in any public context.

Variation XIII

This variation is the only untitled one of the set. In fact, the qualification 'untitled' is not strictly true as Elgar put three asterisks in inverted commas at the head of the variation in place of the initials or names of the others.

This variation is, then, the only one that was impossible to identify. It might be argued that 'Nimrod' was not necessarily that easy either, but the association of Nimrod, 'the mighty hunter', with Jaeger (the German word for 'hunter') was sufficient to enable identification, and already, in 1906, Ernest Newman wrote...

> a little transposition of 'Nimrod' into another tongue will yield the name of a well-known London admirer of the composer.[4]

However, the only person who could reveal the identity of Variation XIII was Elgar himself and we have his identification in his manuscript notes for the pianola roll issue of the *Variations* dating from 1929 (the notes were actually written in 1927):

> The asterisks take the place of the name of Lady Mary Lygon[5]

This statement didn't actually appear in the published version of the notes, which read thus:

The asterisks take the place of the name of a lady who was, at the time of the composition, on a sea voyage.[6]

However, the manuscript is clear.

In fact, Elgar must have revealed her identity to various people over the years and there are various examples of this. For example, in his letter of 2 May 1899 to Jaeger talking about this variation, he says:

The pretty Lady is on the sea & far away...[7]

... using a capital 'L' for 'Lady'.

Much more explicit is the fact that according to Sir Jack Westrup Elgar himself wrote the names of all the 'variants' in Ivor Atkins' copy of the piano duet version of the score and Variation XIII is headed 'Lady Lygon'.[8]

A sort of evidence 'by omission' is that Dorabella never mentions any mystery surrounding the identity of this variation as she surely would have done if Elgar had refused to tell her. The inference is that Elgar did indeed tell her.

Lady Mary herself obviously knew, as can be deduced from a letter Elgar wrote to her on 25 July 1899:

the Variations (especially *** No. 13), have been a great triumph for me under Richter...[9]

In the light of these points, plus the fact that Elgar used Lady Mary's initials to identify the variation in some of his sketches, it doesn't appear that Elgar made any strenuous efforts to hide the identity behind Variation XIII, nor does there seem to be any reason to suspect that Lady Mary Lygon may not have been the real person behind the asterisks.

And yet the question of who was behind Variation XIII has given rise to speculation as no other variation has, and among those to have harboured doubts about Elgar's identification are at least three people who were actually friends of the composer (Rosa Burley, Ivor Atkins and Ernest Newman). Of these, only Ivor Atkins is known to have openly suggested an alternative identification in the person of Helen Weaver,[10] and indeed this name has in recent years been advanced with particular insistence.

Helen was Elgar's fiancée in Worcester in the mid-1880s, but the relationship was never easy because of the difference in religions (Elgar was Roman Catholic), and eventually the engagement was broken off. In the autumn of 1885, Helen emigrated to New Zealand.

Elgar was naturally deeply upset, as his letters of the time to his Yorkshire friend, Charles Buck, show, and this, combined with Helen's long sea voyage, has given rise to a school of thought that she is the real person behind Variation XIII. Elgar, it is argued, could not openly identify his lost love, if only through deference to his wife, and so used Lady Mary Lygon as a sort of front.

I should add that the figure of Helen Weaver, which, to my mind has been over-exaggerated, has also been proposed as the hidden dedicatee of the Violin Concerto.

It is of course perfectly possible that Lady Mary's sea voyage reminded Elgar of Helen's, and that this memory spilled over into the music of the variation, but the inescapable fact is that there is not a shred of evidence to support this idea, whereas we have various supporting arguments in favour of Lady Mary.

All the doubts over the real identity behind Variation XIII seem to arise from four considerations:

1. The fact that Lady Mary was not, as Elgar stated, on a sea voyage at the time the variation was written (she left on 11 April 1899).

2. The nature of the music itself, seen as portraying emotions which go rather beyond friendship

3. The three asterisks, which obviously invite speculation in the same way as the quotation at the head of the Violin Concerto.

4. The fact that the variation is sub-titled 'Romanza'.

Let's look at each of these in turn.

The sea voyage: The idea has been advanced that it is surely conceivable that in his notes, Elgar, writing 29 years after the event, might have made a mistake in his timing and this seems eminently reasonable. The fly in the ointment is that the timing problem dates from much earlier. Ernest Newman in his 1906 book wrote that the variation...

> ... refers to a friend who was crossing the ocean when the Variation was written.[11]

This must have come either directly or indirectly from Elgar himself and it is rather more difficult to imagine timing problems only seven years after the event.

It therefore seems likely that when referring to this variation, Elgar deliberately telescoped the real sequence of events. Why should he have done this? It seems to me possible that his motivation might have been connected with his use of a fragment from Mendelssohn's overture *Calm Sea and Prosperous Voyage* in the music.

Setting aside his various arrangements of other composers' works, I can only think of four other works in which Elgar used fragments of music written by somebody else, and these are *The Apostles, The Music Makers, Polonia* and *The Starlight Express*, all written later. Indeed, he was extremely sensitive to the slightest suggestion of any echo of another composer's work in his own. This sensitivity is very evident in his letters to Jaeger referring specifically to his use of the Mendelssohn fragment in Variation XIII, and at one stage he wanted to cut it out altogether. He explained:

> ...I meant this (originally) as a little quotation from Mendelssohn's Meeresstille ü. Glückliche Fahrt. – but I did not acknowledge it as the critics – if one mentions anything of the kind – talk of nothing else – so I have cut out the reference...[12]

The next day he was even more petulant:

71

I can when in town alter the skore & cut out Meeresstille – I'm in a fit & take no food thinking of your horrid words about another reminiscence. I'm d----d if ever I try to write any more music.[13]

Jaeger evidently persuaded him to leave the Mendelssohn quotation as it was but on all three occasions that the solo clarinet has the tiny two-bar fragment, a pair of quotation marks thus – " " – appears above the music.

If Elgar went to what might appear to us to be such ludicrous lengths to identify his musical quotation, then it is surely plausible that he could have decided to take liberties with the actual timing of Lady Mary's departure in order to 'justify' it.

The nature of the music: Ernest Newman, one of the doubters that Mary Lygon was the 'real' Variation XIII, wrote in 1956:

> a study merely of Elgar's scoring of the variation should make it clear to any person of more than average sensibility that he was here dwelling in imagination on somebody and something the parting from whom and which had at some time or other torn the very heart out of him.[14]

And yet in his 1906 book the same Newman had written of 'the marine picture', and said:

> at the very end the sense of the ship vanishing in the distance is exquisitely conveyed.[15]

I suppose he could have changed his mind, but the score was the same and presumably Newman had studied it prior to his 1906 book.

In fact, the marine nature of the variation is in no doubt, due to the presence of the Mendelssohn quotation which, as we have seen, Elgar went out of his way to point out by putting in quotation marks. The scoring vividly suggests a sea voyage: the famous timpani part evoking the muffled rumbling of the ship's engines, the gently rocking strings (recalling the rhythm of the Enigma theme) suggesting the heave of the swell.

In the final analysis, the reaction to the emotional charge of any music is a completely subjective affair. Indeed, to my ears the music of the preceding variation, Variation XII, is a much more passionate outpouring, especially the *molto espress.* strings in unison with *largamente* woodwind five bars after Figure 54, all double *forte*, followed, four bars later, by an achingly longing phrase on solo cello. In fact the first bars of Variation XIII come as a lighter mood after the intensity of the closing bars of Variation XII.

But nobody, to my knowledge, has ever suggested that Variation XII represents anyone else but Basil Nevinson.

The dangers inherent in drawing any conclusions from the music of any one of the variations are amply illustrated by the Troyte variation:

Arthur Troyte Griffith was a Malvern architect and this music hammers out great blocks of sound as if in preparation for some noble edifice.[16]

... this could play on his 'Ninepin' nickname, touch on his 'maladroit' attempts at the piano or it might refer to a walk taken by the two of them that weekend on the Malverns in a thunderstorm.[17]

It was generally reported of Troyte that he enjoyed argument (perhaps the thrust of the timpani emphasis of the variation?)[18]

Troyte was gifted with a faculty for saying the unexpected. Elgar depicts this characteristic by placing the accents (...) so that a different note becomes accented in each bar.[19]

I never fully understood the 'Troyte' Variation. (...) My recollection of Troyte in the early days was that he used to sit and grin with amusement but say hardly anything.[20]

In his own notes on the subject, Elgar gave the piano version of events, but in the comments I have quoted it is very much a case of 'something for everybody'!

I am reminded of something somebody once said to the effect that a drama critic is a person who surprises a playwright by informing him what he meant.

The three asterisks: In his sketches, Elgar identified the variation with the letter 'L', and in one sketch for the Finale it would appear that he thought of re-using the thematic material of 'L.M.L.' This, obviously, constitutes further evidence in favour of Lady Mary Lygon as the subject of this variation, but at the same time prompts curiosity as to why, if he used her initials at some point to identify the variation, did he decide to abandon them in favour of asterisks.

Dorabella offered the following explanation:

> The composer had written asking permission of Lady Mary to use her initials at the head of No XIII, but as his letter was not in time to catch her before they sailed he decided to replace initials by three asterisks.[21]

It seems to me unlikely that Dorabella made this story up; she may even have been told it by Elgar himself. But the fact is that all the available evidence argues against it.

For a start, Lady Mary left for Australia in early April 1899, a month and a half after the *Variations* had been completed in full orchestration and sent, with the asterisks above Variation XIII, to Vert. If any permission needed to be asked, Elgar would have had ample time before her departure, and indeed, we know from Alice's diary that Lady Mary was actually at the Elgars' home for tea on the very day the score was sent to Vert. He did ask her permission (which was granted) to dedicate the *Three Characteristic Pieces* to her during this period, and on the subject of letters arriving late, it should not be forgotten that we are talking of those far-off days when many letters were delivered the same day they were posted.

Secondly, why would he have needed her permission at all? After all, the initials above the variations are there for identification purposes, they are not dedications as such. And there is no evidence that Elgar asked for anyone else's permission. His letter to Jaeger dated 24 Oct 1898 says simply '... you are Nimrod'. Could it be possible that Lady Mary's titled status led Elgar to act otherwise in her case? Possibly, but unlikely in the light of the other evidence we have.

What seems to me to be the most plausible explanation of the use of the asterisks was in fact hinted at by Elgar himself in his letter of

16 February 1899 to F G Edwards announcing the completion of the *Variations:*

> ... 13 in number (but I call the finale the fourteenth because of the ill-luck attaching to the number)[22]

In the light of this it would seem more than likely that the asterisks were used to avoid associating the number thirteen directly with anybody. Diana McVeagh was, I think, the first to put forward this explanation, in 1977.[23] More recently, Gordon Lee has repeated the same idea, but at the same time added another one, namely that Lady Mary might have refused permission for her initials to be used.[24]

The likelihood of this obviously depends on whether Elgar asked permission at all, and this, as I have already tried to show, is very much open to doubt.

Before leaving this point, it is interesting to reflect for a moment on the subject of Elgar's other dedications to his 'friends pictured within'. As we have just seen. Lady Mary Lygon is the dedicatee of the *Three Characteristic Pieces* but only three other 'variants' have other works dedicated to them and they are Elgar's wife, Isabel Fitton and George Sinclair. This last-named has in fact no fewer than three works dedicated to him if one includes the carol *A Christmas Greeting*, where he shares the dedication with the choristers of Hereford Cathedral, and this makes him, along with Percy Hull (his successor as organist at Hereford), Hubert Leicester (a lifelong friend of Elgar's from his childhood), and God (A.M.D.G.), the record holder among Elgar's dedicatees.

On the other hand, Jaeger never had a work dedicated to him.

The sub-title 'Romanza': Rosa Burley in her book of reminiscences, maintains that Lady Mary Lygon was not the person behind Variation XIII. She wrote that the music of the variation ...

> ... bore no reference to the liner and the sea voyage ... but, as might be expected in a movement called 'Romanza', expressed something very different.[25]

This statement makes the mistake of understanding the term 'Romanza' to indicate that the music has 'romantic' connotations, which is not the case at all. The *Concise Grove* states:

> In the 19th century the term was used for small character-pieces, for example, Schumann's *Drei Romanzen* Op 28.

In fact, the interesting aspect of Variation XIII's sub-title is not its nature but the fact that it should be there at all.

There are four sub-titles in the *Variations*, as follows:

Theme	Enigma
Variation X	Intermezzo
Variation XIII	Romanza
Variation XIV	Finale

Of these, the last is self-explanatory, and we have already looked at the first in Chapter 2. So we are left with the Intermezzo and the Romanza.

On the surface of it, the Intermezzo seems to have a ready explanation, and that is that of all the variations, Elgar thought that this one would be particularly suitable as a piece to be played separately. This is clear from the two letters he wrote to Novello on 13 March 1899: one, addressed 'Dear Sirs', says:

> ... No X e.g. will do well for separate issue [26]

...whilst the other, addressed to Jaeger, states:

> ... the 'pretty' one X shd. do very well as a separate venture – ...[27]

He returned to the subject in his 9 April 1899 letter to Jaeger:

> X (Dorabella) will probably be wanted for separate use[28]

In between times he had also mentioned the possibility of separate publication to Dorabella herself in his letter to her of 26 March 1899.[29]

Although in none of these letters does he refer to the variation as 'Intermezzo', it seems possible that he may have adopted this sub-title to facilitate separate publication along the lines of the *Canto Popolare* from *In the South* or the *Dream Interludes* from *Falstaff*. The same, however, cannot readily be said of the 'Romanza' as there is no evidence that Elgar thought it particularly suitable for separate issue.

On the other hand, it is of course possible that Elgar adopted 'Romanza' for Variation XIII so that it would at least have a title other than simply three asterisks, but if this is so, then the same reasoning cannot be applied to Variation X, which does have a 'normal' title – 'Dorabella'.

It therefore seems to me that if there was a common logic behind these two sub-titles then we must look for it elsewhere, and there is, in fact, another intriguing possibility – somewhat speculative, I must admit, but plausible nonetheless.

Of all the variations, these two are the ones which appear to have little or no connection with the theme. If we refer back to C A Barry's first performance programme note, we find Elgar's statement:

> ... I warn you that the apparent connexion between the Variations and the Theme is often of the slightest texture.

He must have been making a reference to these two variations as all the others without exception have very obvious connections with the theme. In the case of Variation X he was apparently more specific still, as Dorabella tells us:

> E. E. said that there was only a trace of the 'Enigma' theme in the 'Intermezzo' which no one would be likely to find unless he knew where to look for it.[30]

As for Variation XIII, for 31 of its 51 bars it dwells on the Mendelssohn fragment and is therefore not concerned with the Enigma theme. There are of course connections with the theme, although, using Elgar's phraseology, they are of the slightest texture.

Variation X, for instance, starts:

The underlying pattern here is:

... which is a major-key version of the G minor rising arpeggio of the third bar of the 'Enigma' theme...

Whilst in Variation XIII, the rhythmic pattern that the violas have to accompany the Mendelssohn quotation starting one bar after Figure 56 (and repeated later) – two crotchets, two quavers, two quavers, two crotchets – recalls that of the theme, albeit the other way around.

But the fact remains that these two variations are far more remote from the theme than any of the others – which suggests the possibility that they were not originally variations on the theme at all.

This idea, which had been trotting around in the back of my mind for some years, was given new impetus when I read Brian Trowell's study *Elgar's Use of Literature* in which he suggests origins for Variation X that predate the Op 36 *Variations* by some years. Professor Trowell demonstrates how this movement seems to have been planned as an intermezzo in a four-movement suite for strings that never eventually saw the light of day.[31]

If indeed Variation X had, at least partially, origins outside the framework of the 'Enigma' theme, as Variation XIII explicitly did because of the Mendelssohn quotation, could this explain why Elgar chose to mark these variations out with sub-titles? Could they be considered as interpolations in some way offering, in Professor Trowell's words, 'contrast and relief'? The two variations are certainly connected in the sketches as the very first outline of the opening phrase of Variation XIII is to be found on the back of sketches for Variation X.

In any event, if this reasoning is sound, then Elgar must have had it in mind at a very early stage, as Dorabella heard her variation for the first time only 11 days after Elgar's first musings at the piano.

* * * * *

Before leaving the subject of Variation XIII, there is another detail which I ought to mention, although it has implications which go counter to the general direction of my reasoning thus far.

A week after Elgar died in 1934, there was a memorial service in Worcester Cathedral at which the London Symphony Orchestra took part. The music was selected by Ivor Atkins and included the theme and three of the *Variations*, namely C.A.E., 'Nimrod' and '***'.

On one level, the choice of '***' can be understood because the music evokes a long journey, thus echoing the 'Proficiscere, anima Christiana' (Go forth upon thy journey, Christian soul) from *The Dream of Gerontius*, which was also performed as part of the memorial service.

However, bearing in mind that Ivor Atkins was one of the people who was convinced that there was something more behind the three asterisks than Elgar admitted, at least in public, there is another possible interpretation.

If one recognizes that C.A.E. and 'Nimrod' would have been included at least in part because of the immense significance that the people behind the variations, namely Elgar's wife and Jaeger, had in Elgar's life, can one then reasonably assume that the same criterion may well have been behind the choice of '***'?

And if this is a reasonable assumption, could it be that the 'doubters' may be right after all...?

Variation XI

Variation XIII is the only one which has given rise to speculation about the real identity behind the music. However, one other variation has caused speculation, in this case over what the music portrays, and that is Variation XI (G.R.S.), which depicts G R Sinclair, organist at Hereford Cathedral.

In fact Sinclair's identity was one of the easiest to guess, and already in 1906 Ernest Newman could write:

> 'G.R.S.' will be no mystery to any one who knows the names of the 'Three Choir' organists [32]

And when Elgar wrote his notes on the *Variations* in 1927 he was much more detailed on this variation than any other:

> The variation has nothing to do with organs or cathedrals, or, except remotely, with G.R.S. The first few bars were suggested by his great bulldog Dan (a well-known character) falling down the steep bank into the River Wye (bar 1); his paddling up stream to find a landing place (bars 2 & 3); and his rejoicing bark on landing (second half of bar 5). [33]

Understandably, early students of the work, without the benefit of Elgar's explanation or access to the sketches, heard in the bassoons and double basses of bars 2 and 3 a representation of...

> the musician's skill on the pedal-board of his instrument [34]

... as Dunhill put it.

Even before the first performance, *The Sheffield Independent*, referring to Elgar's different treatments of the theme in the individual variations, remarked that ...

> ... a violoncellist might make it an agreeable solo, and that a cathedral organist could embellish it with pedal notes. [35]

But even today, despite all that we now know, the notion that the variation is not about Dan at all but purely about his master's skill on the organ pedals still persists, notably in various writings by Professor

Alice and Edward Elgar
outside their home 'Forli'
Malvern Link, where the
Variations were written.

Alice and Edward
in the mid-1890s

i

Opening page of the full score of the *Variations*, with the word 'Enigma'
added at the top

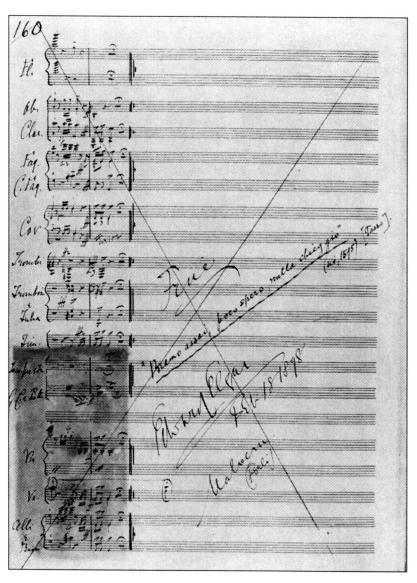

The first ending of the *Variations,* with the Tasso quotation and the wrong completion date.

'My friends pictured within'

George Sinclair with Dan

Richard Arnold

Isabel Fitton

Arthur Troyte Griffith

William Baker

iv

Lady Mary Lygon

Winifred Norbury

August Jaeger

Basil Nevinson

Dora Penny

Hew Steuart Powell

Richard Townshend

Hans Richter (1843-1916)

Richter's letter to his agent Vert,
arranging to give the first
performance of the *Variations*.

Arthur Troyte Griffith at the Elgar
birthplace in 1938.

August Jaeger

George Sinclair with Dan

Dorabella (Mrs Richard Powell) in 1956.

ST. JAMES'S HALL.

RICHTER CONCERTS

UNDER THE DIRECTION OF

MR. N. VERT.

SUMMER SEASON, 1899.
(32nd Series.)

DR. HANS RICHTER, CONDUCTOR.

PROGRAMME

OF THE

FIFTH CONCERT

MONDAY, JUNE 19, AT 8.30.

Vocalist:
Miss MARIE BREMA.

ORCHESTRA OF 100 PERFORMERS.

Leader:
MR. ERNST SCHIEVER.

Director of the Richter Choir:
MR. THEODOR FRANTZEN.

Left and below:
pages from the programme of the
first performance

Programme.

OVERTURE, "Carneval" ... ... *A. Dvořák.*

LEGEND for Orchestra, "Zorahayda" (Op. 11)
J. S. Svendsen.
(First performance at these Concerts.)

CLOSING SCENE from "Götterdämmerung" *Wagner.*
BRÜNNHILDE—MISS MARIE BREMA.

VARIATIONS for Full Orchestra (Op. 36) *Edward Elgar.*
(First performance.)

SUITE pour orchestre, tirée de l'opéra
"Snégourotchka" (" The Snow-Maiden")
N. Rimsky-Korsakow.
(First performance at these Concerts.)

SYMPHONY in D, "Prague" ... ... *Mozart.*

Ian Parrott, who has even gone so far as to describe Elgar's explanation as 'utterly outrageous' and 'a clumsy deception'.[36] Strong words indeed!

But in spite of Professor Parrott's invective, the simple and inescapable fact is that all the available evidence is stacked against him.

For a start, we again have a question of motivation. Why on earth would Elgar invent a story like this, especially one that goes into bar-by-bar detail? Professor Parrott's reasoning on this point is closely connected with his theory that the figure of J S Bach is the hidden theme behind the *Variations* and that the Sinclair variation version of the theme predated the theme itself. For Professor Parrott, therefore, Elgar, who consistently refused to reveal what the hidden theme was, gave a deliberately misleading explanation for the Sinclair variation, designed to act as a smoke-screen to divert attention away from where the truth behind the Enigma was to be found.

Apart from being hopelessly far-fetched, this explanation stands or falls by whether Bach is the hidden theme or not, and, given that he isn't, as we shall see later, the explanation therefore falls.

But even without Elgar's explanation we have clues which point clearly to Dan's involvement in the variation, the clearest one being that in one of the sketches Elgar has written the word 'Dan' over bar 5 which contains the dog's 'rejoicing bark'.

As for the musical phrase representing that bark, Percy Hull pointed out...

This double third passage (bar 5) was quoted in 'Moods of Dan' long before the Variations were written and it was also used in 'King Olaf'... in the accompaniment to the words 'they found the watch-dog in the yard'.[37]

Elgar used to sign Sinclair's visitors' book with musical themes called 'The Moods of Dan', and although in fact Percy Hull was mistaken in saying that the bar 5 bark appears among these themes, another musical bark does, specifically labelled as such, and interestingly enough, it occurs in the inscription dated the weekend of 29 October 1898, the weekend immediately following the emergence of the 'Enigma' theme. It therefore seems plausible to suggest that Dan's excursion into the River Wye occurred during this particular weekend.

A further clue comes from the orchestration of the variation, for apart from joining in the general tumult 13 bars from the very end of the Finale, the triangle has nothing whatsoever to do in any variation except this one, in which it makes three appearances.

Now there is no way in which the triangle can be said to be suggestive of a great cathedral organ. It is, however, extremely suggestive of droplets of water such as might be shaken off a wet dog.

It is clear from the evidence that Dan is involved in this variation, and Elgar's explanation fits in perfectly well with this, as does a slightly different version which he reportedly gave to Leslie Sutton sometime during the 1920s:

> Dan saw a cat and chased it so vigorously that when it jumped onto the parapet of the Wye Bridge at Hereford he was unable to stop, cleared the parapet and splashed into the river. He then swam to the bank and gave one solitary bark of achievement or frustration.[38]

And so, if we are to base our conclusions on the available evidence, we have to conclude that Elgar's explanation is eminently more plausible than any other.

Which does not necessarily mean that Elgar was unaware that his bassoons and double basses in bars 2 and 3 were suggestive of organ pedals. As Billy Reed put it:

> It is quite possible that the composer saw also something in common in these two boon companions, the master and his dog, the one paddling away in the river and the other pedalling away on his organ in the cathedral.[39]

Before leaving this variation, and Dan in particular, it is worth briefly mentioning a minor puzzle associated with him. As I have said, Elgar used to inscribe in Sinclair's visitors' book musical fragments which he called 'The Moods of Dan', the first of which is dated June 5-7 1897. There even exists a photograph, apparently dating from 1896, showing Dan with Sinclair, Elgar and others in the garden of Sinclair's house near Hereford Cathedral.

The puzzle is that these dates predate Dan's date of birth – 6 July 1898 – as given on the gravestone Sinclair provided for him in his garden. As it seems unlikely that there were two Dans, the only explanation to this would seem to be that Sinclair somehow got Dan's birthdate wrong on the gravestone, although the date of his death (1 July 1903) is correct and is confirmed by letters dating from that time.

The gravestone, incidentally, still survives, although it very nearly didn't some ten years ago. The problem was that the house, at 20 Church Street, was in desperate need of repairs. As residence of the Hereford Cathedral organists it had been occupied after Sinclair by his successor, Percy Hull. Hull, however, was obliged to move out around 1930 because of damp problems. For a time part of the house was used by Hereford Conservative Club, but in 1988, in order to finance the necessary repairs, a plan was submitted to the local authority for the construction of shops over the garden area. This was abandoned in the face of a sizeable public outcry, and after one further later development attempt the house was purchased by its present owners, Mr and Mrs Woore, who have done an amazing renovation job on the building, parts of which date from the thirteenth century.[40]

Dan's gravestone is therefore still there, not in its original position[41] but nonetheless still there, in a quiet corner of the garden and well cared for.

A touching final note. The month after Dan's death, Elgar, who was extremely fond of dogs, wrote in Sinclair's visitors' book an ascending scale in the key of E flat, with the words 'Key of S' (for Sinclair) underneath. The seventh note of the scale – D (for Dan) – is missing and underneath the point where it would normally have been Elgar wrote 'alas!'

Notes

1. Moore – *Publishers' Letters* – p 108
2. Maine – p 101
3. Moore – *Publishers' Letters* – p 95
4. Newman – p 135
5. Kennedy – *Portrait* – p 96
6. Notes for the Aeolian Company's 'Duo-Art' pianola rolls of the Variations (1929)
7. Moore – *Publishers' Letters* – p 122
8. Westrup- *Proceedings of the Royal Musical Association* – April 1960, reprinted in Redwood – p 65
9. quoted by John Buttrey – ESN – Sep 77 – p 31
10. Atkins – p 479
11. Newman – p 135
12. Moore – *Publishers' Letters* – p 122
13. Ibid – p 123
14. *Sunday Times* –18 Nov 1956. Quoted in Kennedy – *Portrait* – p 97
15. Newman – p 147
16. J McKay Martin – Sleeve notes for 1959 Sargent/Philharmonia recording (HMV)
17. Moore – Spirit – p 32
18. Young – *Friends Pictured Within – p 102*. Published in Monk (ed) – *Elgar Studies*
19. Reed – *Elgar* – p 154
20. Powell – p 107
21. Ibid – p 115
22. Moore – *Publishers' Letters* – p 108
23. ESN – Jan 1977 – p 31
24. ESJ – Sep 1994 – p 260
25. Burley/Carruthers – p 126
26. Moore – *Publishers' Letters* – p 114
27. Ibid – p 114

28. Ibid – p 119

29. Powell – p 15

30. Ibid – p 15 (fn l)

31. *Elgar's Use of Literature* – p 309 (fn 169). Published in Monk (ed) - *Music and Literature*

32. Newman – p 135

33. Notes for the Aeolian Company's 'Duo-Art' pianola rolls of the *Variations* (1929)

34. Dunhill – p 84

35. 12 June 1899. Article signed 'Musicus'. Newspaper held in Sheffield Central Library.

36. ESJ – Nov 1994 – p 342

37. Powell – p 113

38. Kennedy – *Orchestral Music* – p 26 (fn)

39. Reed – *Elgar* – p 155

40. I am grateful to Geoff and Gill Bradshaw of the West Midlands Branch of the Elgar Society for information on the current state of Sinclair's old house.

41. ESJ – Sep 1991 – p 6

5 – Still More Questions

The timpani part in Variation XIII

If exception is made of the audience joining in *Pomp and Circumstance No 1* at the last night of the Proms on the one hand, and straightforward cuts in the music such as Yehudi Menuhin tells us he sometimes made in the Violin Concerto on the other[1], there are three instances in Elgar's music when what is frequently played is not what he wrote.

Two of these are in the last movement of the Second Symphony – the trumpet high B two bars after figure 49 which is often held over into the following bar, and the occasional inclusion of an organ eight bars after figure 165.

The third one is in the *Variations*, specifically in the timpani part in Variation XIII, one bar after figure 56 and again one bar after figure 60. It is at these points that Elgar introduces his quotation from Mendelssohn's *Calm Sea and Prosperous Voyage*, and to suggest the throbbing of the engines of an ocean liner, Elgar wrote a *ppp* roll for the timpani with the instruction that this was to be played using side-drum sticks.

This instruction is usually ignored in favour of coins near the rim of the drum. The practice originated in the very first rehearsals of the work, and the story has often been told of how Elgar was not fully satisfied by the effect produced by his instruction, and how the timpanist, Charles Henderson, had the idea of using half-crowns instead.

In fact, I would suggest that the idea of using coins had nothing to do with producing a better effect but was the result of the fact that as it is written the timpani part is quite simply unplayable by one player alone (and Elgar did not specify that two players were needed).

The problem is that Elgar keeps the timpani roll going up until the very end of the bar before figure 58 (there is even a crescendo marked on this bar), and on the first beat of the following bar writes the indication 'Naturale', meaning that normal timpani sticks are to be used. There is simply no time allowed for the player to change from side-drum sticks to normal sticks.

This reflects, as James Blades put it:

... either wishful thinking on the part of the great composer, or supreme confidence in the performers of his day[2]

The point of the coins is that they can be gripped between the fourth and fifth fingers of each hand, thus permitting the player to also be holding his normal sticks ready for the return to 'Naturale'. Blades points out that much the same effect can be obtained by using fingernails or thimbles, both methods allowing the sticks to be held more or less normally.

Henderson's idea, then, was not so much designed to produce a better effect as to enable something like the originally intended effect to be achieved.

The astonishing thing about all this is that Elgar, who was so meticulous in his scoring, should have written the passage the way he did in the first place. Michael Kennedy has rightly called it 'a rare miscalculation'.

Equally astonishing is that nobody seems to have spotted it during the process of preparation of the instrumental parts for the first performance. Again, Elgar was meticulous about this and frequently, as on this occasion, had recourse to the help of John Austin, a violinist friend from Worcester, although it should be said that this help was really directed towards checking the parts against the score rather than looking for mistakes in the score itself.

It is not that Elgar was less comfortable writing for timpani than other instruments. For instance, James Blades notes his 'correctness' in giving the small drum first at the tuning change instruction written at the end of the first variation – F in D, B flat in C sharp – because of the two drums to be changed, only the small drum (D) is required in the following variation.[3]

Neither would he have deliberately written something that he knew was unplayable; for instance, he said that the trumpet high B in the last movement of the Second Symphony referred to earlier was not carried over to the following bar in the score because he thought it might be too high to hold.

I can only suggest, therefore, that the 'miscalculation' in the timpani part in Variation XIII was an oversight, and probably had something to do with the incredible speed with which the whole work was orchestrated in Elgar's haste to get it finished and despatched to Richter.

Whatever the explanation, it has to be said that Elgar did not judge it sufficiently important to alter the score during the process of preparation for the printed edition (which took place after the first performance) or at any time thereafter, and so the definitive version of the score that we have still includes the 'impossible' change of sticks, and timpanists still to this day use coins; indeed, audiences have grown so accustomed to this that some concert-goers are convinced that the music was written that way.

James Strebing, timpanist with the City of Birmingham Symphony Orchestra, recalls an amusing result of this:

> When I first joined the CBSO and we had a French conductor [Louis
> Frémaux], I used the other end of cane-handled timp sticks and did a quick
> flip for the change. There were several letters from members of the
> audience pointing out to these uninformed foreigners [James Strebing is
> American] that we were not doing the proper thing that Elgar had
> written!![4]

With regard to the coins now used, given that half-crowns have not been around for a long time now, there is no particular tradition attached to any specific coin; apparently any large coin will do – to quote James Strebing again:

... whatever you have in your pocket and have not spent before the concert...[5]

This comment reminds me of something I read or heard a long time ago, I can't remember where, to the effect that the big problem with the half-crown technique was finding a timpanist rich enough to have two at the same time!

On the other hand, another story, attributed by James Strebing to William Kraft, the American timpanist/composer, has it that at the time of the first performance of the *Variations*, when class values were all-pervading, no self-respecting timpanist would have wanted to be seen clutching side-drum sticks, hence the demonstration of superiority by using half-crowns, in those days an appreciable amount of money.

Donald Hunt, former organist at Worcester Cathedral, recalled a different version of the coins technique and one which it would seem Elgar annotated in his own copy of the score. This involved a penny coin being placed on the skin of the drum and then a roll played with the soft sticks.[6]

Apart from the solutions mentioned in the foregoing paragraphs, the only other way around the problem is quite simply to use two timpanists and this too has been done from time to time.

Before leaving this topic, it is interesting to note that this is not the only instance of an orchestral percussionist coming to Elgar's aid to produce a particular sound, as according to a letter from Elgar to Jaeger dated 27 October 1904, Schroeder, then percussionist of the London Symphony Orchestra, contrived the antique cymbal sound Elgar wanted in *The Apostles* by placing a bell on the end of a stick and hitting it with another stick.[7]

The revision to the finale

The Op 36 *Variations* are unique in Elgar's entire output in that it is the only work to have undergone a major revision after its first performance.

Elgar made substantial changes to some of his works during the process of composition or orchestration, most notably in *The Dream of Gerontius*, and on at least two occasions made adjustments to a finished work after it had been performed (*Froissart* and *Falstaff*). But the addition of a hundred extra bars of music to the Finale of the *Variations* constitutes a radical revision on a scale unparalleled in any other work, and so it is interesting to look at the circumstances which led to this revision.

It is generally accepted that Jaeger was the instigator of it, as he wrote to Elgar just after the first performance strongly suggesting that the Finale should be extended to give the whole work a conclusion of greater importance. It was not the first time that Jaeger had made suggestions to Elgar regarding his music, neither was it to be the last, most famously in the case of *The Dream of Gerontius*, In one case, the *Introduction and Allegro*, Jaeger even seems to have been responsible for the initial idea for the whole work.

However, in all such cases Jaeger's comments were made while Elgar was still working on his music – in other words, before it was actually performed. His first recorded comments about the Finale of the *Variations* come after the first performance.

This is strange, as although Jaeger had not seen this work grow as he did others as he received successive batches of manuscript score from Elgar, he had had access to the music since receiving the piano arrangement in mid-March 1899, three months before the first performance. And he did, in fact, make various suggestions to Elgar before the first performance, amongst others concerning the actual title of the work, as we saw in Chapter 2. But nothing is mentioned about the Finale until after the first performance, not even during the period when the work was in rehearsal (3-19 June).

It is thus tempting to think that the idea of extending the Finale may not have come from Jaeger at all but from Richter, and indeed Jaeger tried to persuade Elgar that this was the case. Elgar, however, was unconvinced, as we can see from his letter to Jaeger dated 30 June 1899:

> I should really like to know <u>how</u> you heard that Richter was disappointed
> – he criticised some of it but not the end...[8]

Richter certainly had ample opportunity to mention the end to Elgar had he wished to, as not only were the two men together just after the first performance, but they also went to dinner together that evening in company with Ivor Atkins and Sir Alexander Mackenzie.

However, Ivor Atkins later told his son, Wulstan, about the events of that day, and his version seems to leave in no doubt that Jaeger was behind the idea of extending the Finale. After the first performance Atkins, Jaeger and Elgar joined Richter in the artists' room, where they started discussing details of the *Variations*:

> ...Jaeger raised the point that the last Variation was too short and that the ending could be stronger: Jaeger appealed to Richter (...) and Richter agreed that (...) the finale of the work could be further developed. Elgar disagreed. (...) Jaeger continued pressing his point about the last Variation.[9]

Whosever idea it was, Elgar didn't like it. He told Troyte Griffith that the original ending was more intimate:

> ...he told me that it meant something of this kind 'Well we have had a very pleasant evening. I am glad to hear what you all think about it. Good night.'[10]

...and as we can see from his letters to Jaeger on the subject, he put up a resistance which was at first stubborn:

> ...the end is good enough for me...[11]

... and later reasoned:

> ...the movement was designed to be concise...[12]

However, a week later he was well into the addition to the Finale:

> I am hoping to send you a sketch of a proposed extended finale: there is
> one phrase wh: I can use again.[13]

...and within days it had been despatched to Jaeger, who expressed approval. Elgar was also pleased:

> You're a trump! I'm heartily glad you like the TAIL, I do now it's done.[14]

He even added a quotation at the end of the score of the revised ending:

> Great is the art of beginning, but greater the art is of ending.

In the light of all this there would seem to be no doubt that the new music, which lasts approximately a minute and a half in performance, was added by Elgar in response to Jaeger's insistent comments, and yet even here there has been speculation as to his underlying motivation.

Jerrold Northrop Moore sees the extra music as the result of the realization on Elgar's part that 'the Enigma was not solved' by the Finale in its original form. Brian Trowell sees omnipresent references to the three descending notes of the Mendelssohn quotation of Variation XIII (thus linking the Finale to Lady Mary Lygon's variation and by extension, according to his theory, to Helen Weaver.) Both Michael Kennedy and Ernest Newman detected the return of the 'Nimrod' theme in the new music.

All this makes me feel rather like the little boy in the story of the emperor's new clothes, as it seems to me that the whole thing is infinitely simpler.

Brian Trowell's suggestion is, I think, untenable quite simply because a descending sequence of three notes is a very basic musical building-block which can be found almost anywhere one chooses to look – from the introduction of *All You Need is Love* by the Beatles to the last phrase of *Oh Come All Ye Faithful* via Beethoven's overture *Leonora number 3*, the Welsh National Anthem and *Three Blind Mice*. If one really wanted to, one could find this phrase scattered throughout the *Variations*:

Theme	Horns	last three notes
Var I	2nd violins	three bars before the end
Var II	2nd violins	seventh bar
Var III	2nd flute	fourth bar
Var IV	Cellos and basses	three bars before end

...and so on. However, I don't think anybody would seriously suggest that all these cases (and the many others I haven't quoted) are deliberate references to the Mendelssohn phrase.

The point is that the phrase is such a commonly occurring one that I can't see how any particular significance can be attached to any single occurrence of it, unless of course, as Elgar did in Variation XIII, special attention is drawn to it.

As for Jerrold Northrop Moore's idea that Elgar was somehow providing a better solution to his Enigma, the degree of plausibility of this depends on whether one believes, as I do, that the problem which confronted him was strictly musical – how to lengthen a movement he didn't initially think could be lengthened? – or whether, as Dr Moore believes, for Elgar this problem...

... might call in question the whole issue of his own music.[15]

Clearly questions such as this cannot be categorically resolved either way. What is, however, beyond doubt is that the way Elgar did get over the problem is masterful, and his new music links seamlessly with what he originally wrote, so it is worth taking a closer look at how he did it.

For example, the balance of the final structure of the movement is so finely calculated that it is almost mathematical.

The first section of the movement, which in broad terms introduces the 'E.D.U.' theme ...

...followed by a passage in which the middle section of the main theme is omnipresent leading to a recapitulation of the 'Nimrod' theme, lasts until Figure 70.

At this point the music returns to its opening bars and restates the 'E.D.U.' theme before recapitulating C.A.E. (Variation I). This leads to an abridged repetition of the middle-section passage and thence to a final statement of 'E.D.U.' and the original ending of the movement seven bars after Figure 76.

In the original version, these two sections were of virtually identical length, each occupying almost exactly one half of the movement in terms of playing time (the second section was ultimately truncated by the addition of the new music).

The underlying thematic structure is symmetrical and can be schematised thus:

E.D.U.—middle section of main theme — Nimrod — E.D.U. — C.A.E.—middle section of main theme — E.D.U.

The extension which Elgar wrote constitutes a third section and it is fascinating to note that its playing time is normally nearly exactly one third of that of the whole movement. This cannot be accidental, and shows how Elgar achieved a balance by writing a new section of the same playing time as each of the two original sections.

In addition, the underlying thematic structure of the new section continues and condenses that of the first two:

Figure 76	E.D.U.
Five bars after 76	'Episode 1'
Figure 78	E.D.U.

Figure 79   'Episode 2'
Figure 81   E.D.U.
Figure 82   Final peroration stating first phrase of Enigma theme

What I have termed 'Episode 1' is unmistakably a recapitulation of the Enigma theme as it appears in G.R.S. (Variation XI) in the brass at Figure 48 and again five bars after Figure 50.

ff

It may be objected to this that G.R.S. (ie, Sinclair) does not appear to have had any particular reason, as did Nimrod and C.A.E., to be singled out to be present in the Finale, and it is indeed possible, although unlikely, that Elgar wasn't even aware of the recapitulation. But there can be no possible doubt about it, as although it is true that the rhythmic pattern is that of the Enigma theme in its original statement right at the beginning of the work, G.R.S. is the only variation in which the theme is stated in this particular rhythmic pattern in the major as in the Finale. Furthermore, the recapitulation is given to the brass and is strongly accented, just as in G.R.S.

Elgar recapitulates three phrases of G.R.S. as in the example given above and then follow fifteen bars in which the falling seventh of the third phrase is repeated in various instruments. This lasts until Figure 78, at which point the rhythmic pattern of E.D.U. reappears.

While all this is going on, two other things are happening, both examples of Elgar's mastery. The first is the addition of an optional organ part to the orchestral texture, thus providing a new depth of sound unheard up until this point. In fact the organ's entry with a pedal B three bars after Figure 76 is a moment keenly listened for by many lovers of this work, myself included.

The other is that Elgar, in order to avoid the music losing impetus, drives it forward by means of a long accelerando lasting all of 23 bars, at the end of which the time-signature is literally double what it was at the start of the movement (semibreve = 84 as opposed to the original minim = 84).

At this point. Figure 79, we arrive at what I called 'Episode 2' above, which is really the emotional climax of the movement. Here we find the following melody:

Dr Moore sees this melody as a combination of the two different parts of the theme of the *Variations* – the six-bar Enigma and the major-key middle section – and for him this constituted the right solution to the Enigma that Elgar was supposedly looking for.

True, the first part of the melody is obviously the first phrase of the Enigma theme in the major key, but it is over what happens next that I disagree with Dr Moore. What happens next is, I think, the phrase which Elgar told Jaeger he could use again and is quite simply the fourth phrase of the Enigma theme, which of all six phrases which constitute the theme is the one least used in the *Variations*.

If we write the two phrases as they appear in the theme side by side, we get:

Transposing the first phrase up into its relative major but leaving the fourth phrase as it is produces:

Ignoring differences in note-values, this is note-for-note the melody of 'Episode 2' and this surely cannot be coincidental. The rest of the development of the melody is entirely based on its second phrase, thus giving even more strength to the idea that it was this phrase that Elgar said he could use again.

After two statements of this melody the music moves via a series of descending fourths recalling the opening of Variation XIII (material from which, it will be recalled, Elgar contemplated using again in the original Finale) to a final statement of E.D.U. and the final peroration requoting the first phrase of the Enigma theme.

Just a minute and a half of extra music (1m 27s in Elgar's own recording) but wrought with such mastery and so finely balanced that there seems to be a sort of inevitability about it as if the Finale had always been that way.

The *Variations* with the revised Finale were first performed at the Worcester Three Choirs Festival in September 1899, the third performance of the work itself. Since then the original Finale has been abandoned, and apart from the fact that the last page of the score showing the original ending was reproduced in Michael Kennedy's book *Elgar Orchestral Music* (on page 27), I know of only two instances of its subsequent use. One of these was in Anthony Goldstone's 1995 recording of the piano version of the *Variations* played on Elgar's own Broadwood piano. The original finale was included as an extra item after the work itself as we know it.

The other was in Sir Frederick Ashton's ballet of the *'Enigma' Variations* at Covent Garden in 1968. On that occasion the work with the original finale was even broadcast by the BBC in a radio performance. In passing, it is interesting to note that Elgar himself, who wrote no specifically ballet music other than the delightful and unjustly neglected fifteen-minute score *The Sanguine Fan*, written in 1917 (a project to write a ballet on a subject from Rabelais in 1903 never materialised), alluded to the possible use of his *Variations* as a ballet in a comment to Troyte Griffith in which he imagined a banqueting hall as the backdrop and a veiled dancer representing the 'Enigma'.

One final point concerning the Finale which I think could serve as a cautionary tale to all those determined to find musical references, hidden or otherwise, in the *Variations*.

Billy Reed tells us how he once pointed out to Elgar that the first violin part at Figure 82 is exactly the same musical phrase (ignoring note-value differences) as the opening of the First Symphony, written ten years later:

> Elgar confessed that he was at a loss to account for it, being quite unaware that the repetition existed until it was pointed out to him.[16]

The quotation from Tasso

At the end of the manuscript orchestral score of the Op 36 *Variations*, Elgar wrote the following and underlined it:

> Bramo assai, poco spero, nulla chieggio

This is followed by the comment '(sic, 1595)' and the name Tasso in square brackets. On the following page, he wrote a translation of this phrase:

> I essay much, I hope little, I ask nothing.

This quotation and its translation raise no fewer than three problems:

1. The line as Elgar gives it is not what Tasso wrote.
2. 1595 is not when he wrote it.
3. It doesn't mean what Elgar says it means.

The line as Tasso wrote it in his *Gerusalemme Liberata*, published in 1581, is in the third person rather than the first, as follows:

> Brama assai, poco spera, nulla chiede.

That Elgar read widely is not open to doubt and thus it seems unlikely that he would not have been familiar with the correct version of the quotation he used. He would probably also have been aware that 1595 was, in fact, the year of Tasso's death and not the year he wrote

Gerusalemme Liberata. As for the mistranslation, Elgar was usually much too fastidious with this sort of thing for it to have been a simple mistake.

Until very recently the only detailed examination of these problems was to be found in Professor Brian Trowell's remarkable study *Elgar's Use of Literature*, which was published in 1993[17] and to which I have already had cause to refer. But in that study, despite some thought-provoking observations. Professor Trowell had to conclude that the matter 'remains an enigma'. However, in the November 1998 issue of the *Elgar Society Journal* he was able at last to provide the answer in an article which conveys perfectly the excitement of the discovery.[18]

The key clue was found by Geoffrey Hodgkins, virtually by accident.[19] Whilst researching a completely different subject, Hodgkins consulted a large account book which had been in Elgar's possession. In this he came across a note which read:

'Bramo assai, poco spero, nulla chieggio' Tasso
see 'Sir Rich Grenville'15 –
Mrs Browning

'Sir Rich Grenville' obviously refers to the naval hero Sir Richard Grenville, who in 1591, in the face of overwhelming odds, attacked a Spanish fleet in his ship the *Revenge*, the name later given by Tennyson to his ballad on the subject. This ballad was set to music by Stanford and, as Hodgkins points out, Elgar actually played in the orchestra which performed the work at the Worcester Three Choirs Festival in 1887. However, Hodgkins could not make any further progress in his exploration of this clue.

He also delved into the Mrs Browning lead, but the only thing he was able to discover, which is intriguing in itself, is that Elizabeth Barrett Browning had used the same Tasso quotation although in its correct form (albeit with an 'e' added before the last phrase, giving 'e nulla chiede') at the beginning other 1826 collection entitled *An Essay on Mind, with other Poems*. Finding himself unable to go any further, Hodgkins passed on his discoveries to Professor Trowell, who, by dint of some diligent hunting in the Bodleian Library in Oxford, finally unearthed the answer to the mystery.

Working in the knowledge that Tennyson's ballad had been closely based on Sir Walter Raleigh's 1591 account of Grenville's sea battle, Trowell hunted for it and found that it had been reprinted in 1871 in an edition to which Elgar would have had ready access and which also included two other accounts of the same battle. Trowell found that one of these, *The Most Honorable Tragedie of Sir Richard Grinvile, Knight* by Gervase Markham, has as a sort of motto on its title page the Tasso quotation in the first person exactly as Elgar uses it, although with no mention of Tasso as the source. Also on the title page is the year the book was first published – 1595.

From this it would seem certain that this was where Elgar found his quotation as not only does it explain his reference to 'Sir Rich Grenville', which by the use of inverted commas suggests a possible book title, but also the year of publication of Markham's book corresponds with the one Elgar appended. His use of square brackets around the name Tasso' would indicate that he is filling in a detail not to be found in his source, whilst his use of the word 'sic' would confirm that he was perfectly aware that the line as he uses it was not exactly what Tasso originally wrote.

A further interesting point is, as Professor Trowell observes, that Elgar may well have felt some affinity with Sir Richard Grenville in the matter of facing up to overwhelming odds, as he was given to complaining that the fates were against him and that his work was to no avail.

Interestingly enough, Professor Trowell also discovered from Elizabeth Barrett Browning's correspondence that she too at one stage considered using the Tasso line in the first person as Elgar did, although there is no way Elgar could have known this. Neither is there any evidence that Mrs Browning was familiar with Gervase Markham's use of the line.

Although these fascinating findings provide the answer to the first two problems mentioned above, we are still left with the question of the mistranslation. 'Bramo assai' does not mean 'I essay much', as Elgar gives, but rather 'I desire much', which is not at all the same thing. Now although the adoption of the first person version of the line as used by Markham is understandable on Elgar's part in order to apply the sentiments to himself, it hardly seems legitimate to change the meaning of the original. However, as it is unlikely that Elgar misunderstood the original, or that he was using somebody else's wrong translation, unaware that it was wrong, we are left with the conclusion that the mistranslation must have been a deliberate, if questionable, 'adjustment' on Elgar's part to make the sentiments match his own more closely.

The date of completion

Unbelievable as it may seem, the last page of the manuscript orchestral score raises yet another question apart from those concerned with the quotation from Tasso, and this is the date given by Elgar as the date of completion of the score.

On this last page, alongside the last two bars of the work with its original ending, Elgar wrote the word 'Fine', then a little lower the quotation from Tasso, then he wrote his name and gave the date 'Feb 18 1898'.

In fact he was a year out as he finished the score on Feb 18 1899.

Most of us need a short period of adaptation at the turn of every year to get used to the new number and I am sure that all of us have at one time or another got it wrong when writing a cheque, for example.

The most likely explanation for Elgar's mistake is, then, that for some reason, six weeks into the new year, he was still having trouble with the new last digit. Arguing against this is the fact that he had already written a number of letters in the first part of the year, and when he mentioned the year (as opposed to simply the day and month, or even simply the day) he doesn't appear to have made a mistake.

This has given rise to at least one theory that the date given at the end of the score of the *Variations* was not a mistake but was deliberate on Elgar's part.

Brian Trowell, citing the fact that he can think of no other Elgar manuscript containing a mistake over the date of completion, suggests that something happened in February 1898 which affected Elgar deeply, which found expression in the Tasso quotation and which led Elgar to use date and quotation at the end of the *Variations* score. In support of this idea, he points to a similar situation concerning a sketch for the Violin Concerto which Elgar presented to Alice Stuart Wortley and her husband which he signed and purposely antedated. Professor Trowell says:

> ... here again it was the date of the initial impulse to compose the first movement that Elgar recorded.[20]

This invites two comments. For a start, there is at least one other instance of Elgar slipping up over the date at the end of a manuscript full score and this is in *The Dream of Gerontius*, where the figure '3' of the date 'August 3 :1900' is clearly written over a figure '4', thus showing that Elgar initially got the date wrong.

Secondly, in the case of the Violin Concerto, we are here talking of a sketch and not the manuscript full score, which bears the correct date of completion (Aug. 5 1910). Furthermore, the sketch in question is of a theme particularly associated with Alice Stuart Wortley which occurs in the first movement of the Concerto and first written down by Elgar on the date he recorded. So the date has nothing to do with the initial impulse to compose the first movement, and the sketch is in fact correctly dated and not antedated.

This being so, this episode has absolutely nothing in common with the question of the wrong date at the end of the *Variations* full score and can therefore shed no light on it.

Another point which argues against Professor Trowell's theory is the fact that Elgar also gave a completion date on the title page of the score, where it is given as 'Feb. 19 1899', which, to complicate matters even further, is not the same day of the month as that given at the end! However, if he was going to use a special date because of its significance for him, surely he would have used it in both places and not just at the end.

Broadly speaking, Elgar's usual practice during this period when he reached the end of a score was to mark the end with the word 'Fine', then a quotation, and then his name, followed by the place and date. One can imagine that this ritual came as a sort of release after the intense concentration and effort needed for the scoring, and that as he accomplished it immediately after writing down the very last notes of the score, his mind was still in the music and thus not on mundane details such as the date. In the case of *Cockaigne*, for instance, he doesn't even bother with the day, writing simply 'March 1901'.

The most plausible explanation of the completion date given at the end of the *Variations* is, therefore, that Elgar quite simply made a mistake.

Notes

1. Menuhin – p 131

2. Blades – p 63

3. Ibid – p 58

4. Letter to the author – 24 April 1998

5. Ibid

6. Ibid

7. Moore – *Publishers' Letters* – p 594

8. Ibid – p 129

9. Atkins – p 40

10. quoted in Young – *Elgar O M* – p 278

11. Moore – *Publishers' Letters* – p 127

12. Ibid – p 128

13. Ibid – p 130

14. Ibid – p 130

15. Moore – *Life* – p 272

16. Reed – *Elgar* – p 157

17. Trowell – *Elgar's Use of Literature*. Published in Monk (ed) – *Music and Literature* – p 182-326

18. ESJ – Nov 1998 – pp 301-304

19. Ibid – p 300

20. Trowell – *Elgar's Use of Literature* – p 309 (fn 162). Published in Monk (ed) – *Music and Literature*

6 – *The Hidden Theme*

The terms of the puzzle

And so we come to the question of the hidden theme itself, for it is this aspect of the Op 36 *Variations* more than any other which has attracted interest and speculation over the years. Dorabella said:

> I almost lay awake at night thinking and puzzling, and all to no purpose whatever.[1]

... and I am sure many Elgarians have done the same.

In 1953 the American magazine *Saturday Review* even organized a competition, inviting its readers to send in suggestions as to the identity of the hidden theme.

As Michael Kennedy put it:

> Enigma-solving is a game Elgarians will play to the end of time.[2]

In this study I have laid great emphasis on the importance of respecting the evidence we have at our disposal as being the only acceptable approach. With this in mind, before considering what the hidden theme might be, it is necessary to establish what the parameters are as they can be deduced from the available evidence.

These parameters are as follows:

1. As we have seen earlier in this study, all the evidence points to a musical and not an abstract theme.

2. Again as we have seen, that musical theme must be a counterpoint to the 'Enigma' theme, defined as the first six bars of the *Variations*.

3. It must be well known, as per Elgar's statement:

> it is so well known that it is extraordinary that no-one has spotted it [3]

4. It must have some notes repeated, as we saw in the episode of the sticky labels placed on the piano keys for Troyte's benefit.

5. It must be a theme which Dorabella 'of all people' might have been expected to guess.

6. It is probably a 'popular' theme (for, as we have seen, had it been a theme by Beethoven, for instance, Elgar would surely not have been as reluctant as he was to reveal its identity).

7. It is in all likelihood a theme which Elgar had fresh in his memory.

If we now apply these parameters to the various solutions which have been proposed, we will see that all of them, except possibly one alone, must be discarded.

Analysis of previous solutions

It is impossible to identify all the solutions that have been put forward over the years for the simple reason that there must have been many suggested verbally to Elgar during his lifetime but which have never been recorded.
Dorabella tried:

> I suggested all sorts of tunes trying to see if I could get a rise out of him, or even a hint ...[4]

...but she doesn't tell us what her suggestions were.
Winifred Norbury also tried:

I always consider that I know the hidden tune in the Enigma, but he said I was wrong when I told him.[5]

... but she doesn't tell us what her tune was either.
Troyte also tried and at least he identified his attempt:

When I was visiting Elgar at Kempsey I asked him 'Can I have one guess? Is it God save the King?'[6]

This suggestion dates from 1924, when Elgar was living at Napleton Grange in Kempsey, just outside Worcester, but it seems to me inconceivable that this was Troyte's one and only attempt. He must surely have tried other possibilities a lot earlier, for instance, at the time of the 'sticky labels' episode.

One other suggestion made to Elgar during his lifetime has turned out to be the most persistent of all, and that is *Auld Lang Syne*. In fact we owe the first recorded mention of this solution to Elgar himself in a short but oft-quoted postcard:

No, Auld Lang Syne won't do.[7]

This was written in 1929 to Dyneley Hussey, but in 1934 Richard Powell (Dorabella's husband) published an article which he said was actually written in 1920 in which he too suggests *Auld Lang Syne*.[8] If this is so, then *Auld Lang Syne* is the earliest solution of which we have evidence, and dates from twenty-one years after the first performance of the *Variations*.

Elgar's death in 1934 obviously removed the possibility of would-be enigma solvers trying their attempts directly on the composer himself. Subsequent attempts, therefore, have been channelled through a variety of publications and are thus easier to track. A summary of all the suggestions I have been able to locate is given below.

1920 *Auld Lang Syne* – Richard Powell, published 1934
1924 *God Save the King* – Troyte Griffith, letter 1937
1939 Love, friendship – Ernest Newman[9]
1939 *Nocturne* in G minor (Chopin) – Eric Blom[10]

1939 A melodic framework in Elgar's mind – Billy Reed[11]

1953 *Saturday Review* Competition:[12]

> *Una bella serenata (Così fan Tutte)*
> *Agnus Dei* from B minor mass (Bach)
> *Pathétique* sonata (Beethoven)
> *When I am laid in earth* (Purcell)
> *None shall part us from each other* (Sullivan)

1959 Elgar's 'search for self-discovery' – J Northrop Moore[13]

1960 *Eli, Eli, lama sabachthani* from the St Matthew Passion (Bach) – Jack Westrup[14]

1970 A simple scale – Michael Kennedy[15]

1971 J S Bach – Ian Parrott[16]

1974 *Rule, Britannia* (and, by extension, Britain) – Theodore van Houten[17]

1976 *Ave Maris Stella* (John Dunstable) – Robert E Laversuch[18]

1977 *Prague* Symphony (Mozart) – J M Nosworthy[19]

1977 *Benedictus* from Stanford's Requiem – Raymond Leppard[20]

1979 *Dies Irae* from Catholic Requiem Mass – Ben Kingdon[21]

1984 *Four Serious Songs* (Brahms) – Ulrik Skouenborg[22]

1990 The bicycle – Percy Young[23]

1993 Six octave E's – Brian Trowell[24]

1994 *Hearts of Oak* – Charles Ross[25]

1997 Meditation from *The Light of Life* (Elgar) – J M Rollett[26]

1997 *La Rédemption* (Gounod) – Rodney Stenning Edgecombe[27]

1998 *Te Deum* (Berlioz) – Batya Swift Yasgur[28]

I should stress that this list only records the first mention of the various suggested solutions as some of them have been repeated and developed by subsequent writers on the subject, with *Auld Lang Syne* and the *Dies Irae* theme to the fore in this respect.

Other solutions have been referred to in various sources but I have been unable to determine their exact origin. These are:

- the line of the Malvern Hills
- *Home Sweet Home*
- *Ta-ra-ra-boom-de-ay*
- *All through the night*
- *Pop goes the weasel*
- *For he's a jolly good fellow*

Also deserving of mention, although not really a 'solution' in the sense of a hidden theme, is Christopher Seaman's discovery of a musical acrostic which over the first bar and a half of the 'Enigma' theme spells out 'A CARICE' (to Carice).[29]

Having identified on the one hand the parameters which have to be satisfied, and on the other the solutions proposed to date, it is now possible to see how the latter measure up to the former. The results of this analysis are strikingly clear-cut.

The first parameter excludes all abstract solutions such as friendship, the line of the Malvern Hills, Britain, J S Bach, and so forth.

The second parameter excludes all musical solutions except two. For example, *Auld Lang Syne*, the most famous of all the proposed solutions, only 'goes' with the first four bars, and even then an effort of imagination is necessary.

Any solution which only 'matches' part of the theme, for instance *Rule Britannia* and in particular the 'never, never, never' motif, or Mozart's *Prague* Symphony, can in no way be considered a true counterpoint.

The most recent suggestions are even further away, and the same applies to the prizewinners in the 1953 *Saturday Review* competition.

One of the musical solutions which satisfies the counterpoint parameter is Brian Trowell's idea that the hidden theme was a series of octave E's (representing E E = Edward Elgar) played on the first beat of the first six bars. True it fits, but it is what he himself calls an 'unusual' counterpoint. But this idea falls foul of the need for the hidden theme to be a well-known popular one, quite apart from the implication that for it to be the solution, the 'Enigma' theme must originally have been written in E minor rather than G minor for which there is absolutely no evidence.

The only solution thus far proposed which seems to satisfy all the parameters is the *Dies Irae* theme from the Roman Catholic requiem mass. This was first put forward by Ben Kingdon in 1979 but Mr Kingdon did not propose it as a counterpoint, only as a theme whose notes could be found 'embedded' in the 'Enigma' theme.

It was some years later, in 1986, that Kenneth Kemsey-Bourne proposed the *Dies Irae* theme as a counterpoint (apparently unaware of Ben Kingdon's earlier article as it is not mentioned).[30]

In Mr Kemsey-Bourne's own words, there is a 'fair fit', which is an achievement in itself as no other real theme (as opposed to Brian Trowell's octave E's) has ever come close. However, there are two problems. One is that the last note of the *Dies Irae* theme falls on the first beat of bar seven of the 'Enigma' theme, ie after the double bar. The other is that the fit only applies to the sequence of notes of the 'Enigma' theme and does not extend to Elgar's harmonization of it, which one would have expected had the *Dies Irae* theme really been the hidden theme.

When we consider the other parameters, the *Dies Irae* could fit most of them, although it is clearly not a 'popular' theme, and it is debatable how well known it would have been to non-catholics.

However, this solution is the only one proposed to date that stands up reasonably well to virtually all of the parameters identified earlier. And this paucity of serious candidates has led many people to conclude that perhaps there is nothing in all this after all. Already nearly thirty years ago Roger Fiske observed wistfully ...

> ... how very hard it is to find anything that will go with Elgar's theme even badly...[31]

And yet...

A new solution

And yet there is a tune which fits all the parameters perfectly. Not only does it 'go' in perfect counterpoint with the 'Enigma' theme, but it also sounds completely natural with Elgar's harmonization of it.

And it does all this with absolutely no manipulation. No fooling around with note values, no turning intervals upside down, nothing. And on top of this, the fact that the tune in question is not associated with any specific key in particular means there is no problem on that score either.

The one and only adjustment necessary, given that it is a major-key tune, is to play it in the minor.

That tune is the nursery rhyme *Twinkle, twinkle little star*.

Here it is over the 'Enigma' theme with Elgar's piano score harmony:

After playing this two or three times, or humming *Twinkle, twinkle little star* (henceforth *TTLS* for short) over a recording of the 'Enigma' theme, it is striking how natural it sounds. There is a certain inevitability about it, and the first two bars even sound very reminiscent of the opening of Dvořák's *Slavonic Dance* No. 2 in E minor from the Op 72 set.

There can be no doubt whatsoever that it 'goes', and indeed it seems so 'obvious' that one can fully appreciate Elgar's conviction that someone would spot it and his later astonishment that nobody did. As far as the other parameters are concerned, *TTLS* is clearly well-known and 'popular', and not only does it have repeated notes, the whole structure of the tune is a series of repeated notes.

TTLS could well have been fresh in Elgar's memory as he had been out giving violin lessons on the day he first played the *Variations* theme to his wife, and *TTLS* is exactly the sort of simple tune which violin beginners are given to scrape away at.

The question of 'Dorabella of all people' is fascinating. On one level she might have been expected to guess correctly, possibly because she was the youngest of Elgar's close friends, not long out of school when they first met in late 1895, and thus the closest to childhood. He even referred to her as 'my child' from time to time. Another possible reason why she might have been expected to find the solution, whether it be *TTLS* or not, is that of all Elgar's closest friends at the time of writing the *Variations*, she was probably the most actively musical. As she herself tells us:

> I was so mixed up with tunes in those days; Choral music, Church music, and orchestral music – and then my own solo singing, scenes from opera, songs, ballads, and so on.[32]

She, of all people, could have been expected to spot a counterpoint.

But there is another dimension to the relationship between Elgar and Dorabella which it seems to me is key in all this. As I have already said, she was the youngest of Elgar's close friends at the time of the *Variations*, and, if we take her recollections at face value, as there seems no reason not to do, then Elgar was with her at his most playful. The child-like, mischievous element in him could find expression in her company in a way impossible to imagine with his wife, or indeed with pretty well all of his other acquaintances at that time, and she got to know and enjoy this facet of his character. He liked, as she says, 'fun and nonsense'.

This surfaces on many occasions in Dorabella's book, amongst others when she talks of how his humour found expression in music, his setting of the football commentary 'he banged the leather for goal' for instance.

She tells us of his less 'serious' musical activities:

> ... at other times he played all sorts of amusing things; bits from this and that, old songs, nursery rhymes – altered to suit his mood or in imitation of some other composer.[33]

'...nursery rhymes – altered to suit his mood or in imitation of some other...' If *TTLS* is the hidden theme, then in this short phrase Dorabella has precisely described the Op 36 *Variations*. It can thus almost be said that the solution to the 'Enigma' has been virtually staring us in the face since the first publication of Dorabella's book over sixty years ago. Knowing the 'fun and nonsense' side of Elgar as she did, then she of all people should have been able to guess.

So the first conclusion that can be drawn is that *TTLS* fits the known criteria in a way that no other solution suggested to date has done. For this reason alone it has to be taken seriously as a possible solution to the 'Enigma'.

But there is more, for it turns out that there is an astonishingly close relationship between *TTLS* and the middle section of the *Variations* theme. This middle section consists of four phrases of near identical structure. This structure is a sequence of four ascending notes followed by a descending fourth in the first two phrases and a descending fifth in the other two. Of the six phrases which constitute *TTLS*, four are a sequence of four descending notes whilst the two others start with an ascending sixth, which, if you move the first note up an octave, becomes a descending fourth.

The relationship is so close that the middle section of the *Variations* theme, whilst not a counterpoint on *TTLS*, can be considered a true variation of it. This being so, wherever the *Variations* echo the middle section of the theme, they are by extension also echoing *TTLS*.

This can be seen again and again, most notably in Variation V, where the pattern of four descending notes can be found in the violins five times in the first six bars, and many other times subsequently. Or again in the Finale following Fig 66, where descending four-note sequences can be found in one instrument or another for no less than eighteen of the following twenty bars. And following the blaze at Fig 82 there is a 'slow-motion' descending four-note sequence extending over eight bars.

Clearly, if the 'Enigma' part of the theme is a counterpoint on *TTLS* whilst the middle section of the theme is a variation on it, then Elgar's phrase...

... through and over the whole set another and larger theme 'goes'...

...becomes obvious, for on the one hand, through the two contrasting sections of the *Variations* theme *TTLS* is omnipresent, whilst it is a 'larger' theme in the sense that it embraces both parts of the *Variations* theme.

If *TTLS* is in fact the hidden theme, then all sorts of things fall neatly into place including, possibly, the choice of the very word 'enigma', for the second line of *TTLS* – 'how I wonder what you are' – is indeed strongly suggestive of an enigma.

In addition, *TTLS* is a very well-known tune and fits naturally the 'Enigma' theme. We can now therefore understand why Elgar was so sure someone would find it and thus why, in order to avoid any possible embarrassment, he stopped calling his theme an 'original' theme and started, via the enigma mechanism, acknowledging that there was a hidden theme.

What were his alternatives? Calling his Op 36 'Variations on *Twinkle, twinkle little star*' would hardly have helped at a time when he was still struggling to build up a reputation as a serious composer and when he still felt that the London musical establishment was hostile to him.

He could have used the French version of the rhyme – *Ah! vous dirai-je Maman* – but Mozart had already done this. In fact, the French version could well have been in Elgar's mind when he was sat at the piano improvising. The first two lines of the French text run as follows:

> Ah! vous dirai-je Maman
> Ce qui cause mon tourment.
> (Ah! I will tell you Mummy
> What is the cause of my anguish.)[34]

This sentiment could well have applied to Elgar himself given his depressed state of mind on that October evening, and even if Elgar was not familiar with the second line of the French version, at the very least this is a fascinating coincidence.

He could have used *Variations on a Nursery Theme*, as Dohnanyi later did, but Dohnanyi's work is deliberately humorous and thus invites a smile. (Incidentally, it is interesting to note in passing that apart from Mozart and Dohnanyi already referred to, the melody of *TTLS* was also used as a theme for variations by Adam and Grétry, whilst Saint-Saëns quoted it in *Carnival of the Animals*, and so it can be said to have a certain 'pedigree' in classical music!)

But in any case, any of these alternatives would have more or less obliged Elgar to state *TTLS* at the beginning of his Op 36, and this would clearly neither have been acceptable nor appropriate for, as we have seen in an earlier chapter, Elgar's work is in effect a set of variations on a variation on a theme, and even if *TTLS* is the origin of it all, the 'Enigma' theme is the motor.

So the solution found by Elgar, or Jaeger, or both, emerges as the best in the circumstances, and what they did now has a perfectly clear and natural explanation.

As have Elgar's changing attitudes to the hidden theme over the years, at first almost encouraging Dorabella to rack her brains, and teasing Troyte with the sticky labels, later becoming much more reticent. As it became clear that the hidden theme was proving more elusive than Elgar had anticipated, so he gradually started to suspect that it would never be found, and as he did not really want to reveal it in the first place, so he avoided the topic.

And he was right, for the plain truth is that in the context of the music of the Op 36 *Variations*, the hidden theme is irrelevant. *TTLS* has no bearing whatsoever on the nature of the music other than to have opened the door to inspiration. If Elgar had not mentioned it, nobody would have looked for a hidden theme, and by mentioning it, albeit, as I have suggested, as a sort of insurance policy, so he invited speculation.

Notes

1. Powell – p 119
2. Kennedy – *Portrait* – p 86
3. quoted in Powell – p 119
4. Powell – p 120
5. quoted in Powell – p 120
6. quoted in Powell – p 119
7. quoted in A H Fox Strangways – *Music and Letters* – Jan 1935. Reprinted in Redwood – p 58
8. *Music and Letters* – July 1934. Reprinted in Redwood – pp 50-55
9. *Sunday Times* – 16 Apr – 17 May 1939
10. Reed – *Elgar* – p 52 (fn l)
11. Ibid – p 153
12. Westrup – Proceedings of the Royal Musical Association – 23 Apr 1960 Reprinted in Redwood pp 60 – 75
13. *Musical Review* – Feb 1959 – pp 38-44
14. See note 12
15. Kennedy – *Orchestral Music* – p 22
16. Parrott – p 49
17. ESN – Sept 1974 – p 15

18. ESN – Jan 76 – p 22

19. Letter to *Daily Telegraph* – 27 Mar 77 Quoted by Ian Parrott in ESJ –
    May 92 – p 9

20. *The Times* – 20 Aug 1977

21. ESJ – May 1979 – pp 9 – 12

22. *Music Review* – Vol. 43 – pp161 – 168

23. Young – 'Friends Pictured Within' – p 99: published in Monk (ed) –
    Elgar Studies

24. Trowell – 'Elgar's Use of Literature' – p 306 (fn 147): published in Monk
    (ed) – Music and Literature

25. ESJ – Sep 1994 – pp 265-269

26. ESJ – Nov 1997 – pp 106-122

27. ESJ – Nov 1997 – pp 124-127

28. *Elgar Society News* – Nov 1998 – p 4

29. CD notes – National Youth Orchestra of Great Britain/Seaman
    recording – (IMP Classics 1994)

30. ESJ – Sep 1986 – pp 9-12

31. *Musical Times* – Nov 1969. Reprinted in Redwood – pp 76-81

32. Powell – p 119

33. Ibid – p 123

34. I am grateful to my 10-year-old son Andrew for tracking down the full
    French text for me.

7 – Reconstruction of Events

A tried and trusted technique in police investigation is that of reconstruction of events at the scene of the crime. This is done using available evidence to try to shed light on what actually happened, and to test out hypotheses to see if they hold water.

It is illuminating to apply this technique to the evening of 21 October 1898 on the basis of what we know and the ideas that have been put forward in this study, for I submit that the picture that emerges is wholly convincing.

Elgar came home after a day's violin teaching. It was an occupation that he hated and he must have keenly felt the irony of having been fêted after the success of the first performance of *Caractacus* at Leeds just a month earlier, only to have to return to the grind of giving violin lessons. It is hardly surprising that he had been feeling depressed for the last few days. Just the day before he had written to Jaeger:

I tell you I am sick of it all.[1]

On top of which it had very probably been raining. This can be deduced from a comment he made in a letter he wrote to Jaeger three days later:

our woods look lovely but decidedly damp[2]

...and in fact Alice's diary entry for that day says 'wet and warm'.

Elgar was, then, in rather low spirits.

After the evening meal, Alice suggested a cigar to try to cheer him up a little, and having lit it, and feeling 'soothed and relaxed', he sat himself at the piano and started to play nothing in particular, his mind wandering off on other things.

The tune of *Twinkle, twinkle little star* drifted into his consciousness. He may well have heard some eight-year-old violin beginner scraping away at it earlier that day.

Matching his mood, he played a series of chords harmonizing with *TTLS* in the minor but without actually playing the tune itself. And then, in the manner of a passacaglia, he started to embroider on the harmonies he had played. At some point, the six-bar 'Enigma' theme emerged and caught Alice's attention.

> 'Edward, that's a good tune.'
> 'Eh! tune, what tune?'
> 'Play it again. I like that tune.' [3]

Elgar, whose mind had been wandering, had some trouble getting back to the tune that Alice had noticed:

> I played and strummed and played and then she exclaimed:
> 'That's the tune.' [4]

He explained to his wife that it really wasn't a tune at all, but simply an improvisation deriving from his minor-key harmonization of *TTLS*.

Alice was surprised that something deriving from *TTLS* should sound so despondent, to which Elgar responded that that was the way he felt. Anybody else sat at the piano at that moment would have seen it differently:

> Nevinson would have looked at it like this.[5]

He then played a 'Nevinson' version, not of *TTLS*, but of the tune he had derived from it.

This gave him an idea, and it was probably from that moment that his spirits began to rise, for he started to imagine other versions but instead of telling Alice whose they were, he started playing guessing games with her:

> Whom does that remind you of?[6]

... he asked her, having played a version of W.M.B.

I cannot quite say... You are doing something which I think has never been done before.[7]

To which he replied:

...something might be made of it.[8]

He tried one or two others in fairly quick succession, H.D.S-P., for example. Possibly also C.A.E. – Alice's variation – as, apart from the fact that she was in the room with him, her variation and the three already mentioned are the closest to Elgar's theme and share its G minor tonality.

And so the idea took root. And probably not an hour had passed since Elgar had sat down at the piano.

Thus was the hare set running.

Notes

1. Moore – *Publishers' Letters* – p 93

2. Ibid – p 95

3. Forsyth – p 243

4. Ibid

5. Maine – p 101

6. Forsyth – p243

7. Maine – p 101

8. Ibid

8 - *Conclusion*

So is *Twinkle, Twinkle Little Star* the long-sought solution to Elgar's enigma? Obviously, unless the explanation is in an envelope locked away in some lawyer's safe somewhere, we shall never know for sure. However, the arguments I have put forward, both musical and otherwise, are compelling. It can also be said that despite all the efforts of so many people, musicians and laymen, it has taken a hundred years to come up with just one tune which really fits, not only Elgar's theme but also all the other various parameters, whilst at the same time shedding light on some hitherto obscure aspects. The likelihood of there being another tune which does all these things just as convincingly seems to me remote.

But at the end of the day, 'through and over' all the evidence, the arguments and the hypotheses towers the music itself, a work which Michael Kennedy has called:

the greatest orchestral work yet written by an Englishman[1]

And that music has other unfathomable mysteries.

For example, I agree wholeheartedly with Michael De-la-Noy when he says:

it is hard to imagine how Jaeger (...) ever sat through performances of the work knowing that 'Nimrod' had been written for him.[2]

Jaeger lived and breathed music and was especially drawn to Elgar's. What must he have felt listening to what Percy Young has described as:

... one of the simplest and most moving utterances in the whole of music.[3]

Elgar himself left a rather less exalted description in a letter to Jaeger in 1906 in which he said that the variation was:

... written by one Ass to the glorification of another old duck.[4]

Another mystery. I have never really known what to make of C.A.E., the variation portraying Elgar's wife. Of the five 'female' variations it is the only one in the minor, which creates a serious atmosphere which to me at times even suggests a sort of dark foreboding. Elgar described it as:

a prolongation of the theme with what I wished to be romantic and delicate additions.[5]

Dorabella saw it as:

very serene and lovely – and in some curious way like her.[6]

The end is certainly serene but the rest seems to me to be somehow ambiguous and uncertain. I wonder what Alice made of it.

But the greatest mystery of all is how did Elgar, with no large-scale orchestral work behind him (if one excepts *Froissart*), produce in the space of just four months one of his greatest masterpieces? Or, come to that, how did the man produce music like that at all?

Like all Elgarians, I imagine, I never cease to wonder what it was about Elgar that enabled him to produce music which succeeds in moving me in a way in which no other music does. What is the strange alchemy that draws people to his music and, once drawn, traps them?

Whatever it is, it has always been the case. Arthur C Benson wrote in a letter to Elgar dated 24 June 1906:

I can't conceive the process by which you dreamed of such sounds, such textures.[7]

Which puts the mystery in a nutshell.

But it is Elgar's friend Frank Schuster, in a letter to Elgar in 1903 concerning *The Dream of Gerontius*, who comes closest to expressing my own feelings on this:

... I can never forget that you have written (...) and I have only listened (...)! - the gap awes me.[8]

Notes

1. Kennedy – *Portrait* – p 100

2. De-la-Noy – p 73

3. Young – p 283

4. Moore – *Publishers' Letters* – p 650

5. Notes for the Aeolian Company's 'Duo-Art' pianola rolls of the *Variations* (1929)

6. Powell – p 12

7. Moore – *Lifetime Letters* – p 176

8. Moore – *Spirit* – p 41

Appendix 1

Another theme which 'goes'

I have already had cause to quote Roger Fiske's despairing comment in which he laments:

> ... how very hard it is to find anything that will go with Elgar's theme even badly...

In the light of this, I feel particularly favoured by the Gods as in the course of my reflections on the *Variations* I have come across not just one tune which 'goes' but two.

We looked at the first of these – *Twinkle, twinkle little star* – in Chapter 6. The other one, although highly unlikely to have anything to do with the hidden theme, is still worth mentioning if only for its curiosity value.

It is *Ol' Man River* from Jerome Kern's musical *Show Boat*.

This tune, transposed into G minor (the original is in E flat major – Nimrod's key), and combined with the 'Enigma' theme gives the following:

There is no doubt about it – *Ol' Man River* (*OMR* from here on) fits. Or to be more precise, the two tunes fit, as, like the *Dies Irae* theme, *OMR* does not fit Elgar's harmonization of the 'Enigma' theme in the same way that *TTLS* does. Also like the *Dies Irae* theme the last note of *OMR* spills over into bar seven of the 'Enigma' theme.

It is interesting to note that at (A) in the quotation above, both tunes form the same interval of a seventh which occurs in the 'Enigma' theme just afterwards and which is always considered to be so typical of Elgar.

Further examination reveals more interesting similarities between the two tunes, perhaps the most obvious being the pattern of note values which are extremely closely related.

OMR is a series of identical phrases consisting of two crotchets, a quaver and a crotchet with afinal quaver leading into the following bar where the same pattern is repeated. The 'Enigma' theme is a series of phrases consisting of a rest followed by two quavers and two crotchets with the following bar reversing the pattern into a rest followed by two crotchets and two quavers. Despite this close similarity of phrase structure the two quavers of the 'Enigma' theme never occur at the same time as the quaver and the crotchet in *OMR*, always falling just before or just after, producing a musically satisfying effect.

From this it is clear that we are not just dealing with a theme that fits the 'Enigma' theme but with one very closely related to it, and which, when the two are combined together, produces a single perfectly homogeneous and integrated musical passage.

Clearly, as *OMR* was written some thirty years after the Op 36 *Variations*, it cannot be the hidden theme behind Elgar's 'Enigma' theme. This therefore leaves three possibilities:

1.   *OMR* is derived from the 'Enigma' theme.

2.   Both themes are derived from a common earlier theme.

3.   The whole thing is coincidence.

I should perhaps say at the outset that my own view is that we are dealing here with a coincidence. However, the correspondence between the two themes is so close that it is worthwhile to briefly consider the two other possibilities.

Jerome Kern was born in New York in 1885 and so would have been just 14 when the *Variations* were first performed in London. He arrived in London for the first time just four years later, thus starting what Gerald Bordman has called:

...the beginning of a life-long romance with England and the English.[1]

No records exist concerning Kern's activities in London during his 1903-4 stay but it seems logical to suppose that he would have immersed himself in the world of theatre and entertainment.

In 1905 he was back in London again and indeed over the following six years or so he was constantly shuttling back and forth across the Atlantic. In 1909 he met his future wife, Eva Leale, the daughter of a pub/hotel manager in Walton-on-Thames, and in October 1910 they were married.

Now these years, as J B Priestley has put it, were Elgar's, and it is thus inconceivable that Kern, active as he was in the London musical scene of the time, albeit at the popular end of the spectrum, should have been unaware of Elgar and his music. Kern's musical tastes included classical music and he kept busts of Mozart and Wagner on his piano. He is also reported as having tears streaming down his cheeks when listening to one of Toscanini's concerts, and it would even appear that he included a quotation from Richard Strauss's *Der Rosenkavalier* in the piano part for his song *Our Lovely Rose*.

It is highly likely, therefore, that he would have been exposed to Elgar's music.

Intriguingly, he was twice sued for plagiarism. On the first occasion, in 1923, it was for having allegedly 'lifted' the accompaniment of one of his songs from a composition by somebody else. Part of the judge's summing up makes fascinating reading in the present context:

126

Whether he [ie, Kern] unconsciously copied the figure, he cannot say, and does not try to. Everything registers somewhere in our memories, and no one can tell what may evoke it. On the whole, my belief is that, in composing the accompaniment (...) Mr. Kern must have followed, probably unconsciously, what he had certainly often heard only a short time before. I cannot really see how else to account for a similarity, which amounts to identity.[2]

As I said above, I do not believe that *OMR* has Elgar's 'Enigma' theme as its own hidden theme, but nonetheless Kern's connections with, and frequent stays in, England, combined with the other points I have mentioned, show that such a relationship, whilst improbable, could have been possible.

There has in fact long existed a suspicion that Kern's song derived from an earlier melody, but it has been commonly supposed that that melody forms part of some forgotten negro tradition.

Michael Freedland tells how the black chorus at the Philadelphia try-out of *Show Boat* before its New York opening in December 1927 paid Kern an unexpected compliment:

... the singers and dancers told him that they could not understand how a white man could possibly produce music like that of 'Ol' Man River'. Several were sure they'd heard the song when they were children.[3]

Freedland also tells how both Kern and Oscar Hammerstein, the lyricist, sought out every show boat they could find and soaked up the atmosphere. They heard singing on the river banks:

The rhythms stayed with him all the way back home, where the first thing he did was to go to the piano and tap out the one particular melody that had haunted him all the time.[4]

The result was *Ol' Man River*, which could thus, apparently, even if only partially, have been inspired by some authentic negro melody.

Elgar, in his days as Musical Director at the Powick Asylum just outside Worcester, had a contract which stipulated, amongst other things, the writing of accompaniments for Christy minstrel songs. These were very popular at the time and there was an active group of

Christy Minstrels in Worcester, one of whose concerts in 1878 included an Introductory Overture 'written expressly for the occasion' by Elgar himself.

As far as Elgar's attitude to this sort of music is concerned, we have the testimony of Billy Reed and Dorabella that his likes and dislikes covered a wide range of music. Billy Reed tells us:

> Some of the later jazz records fascinated him to such an extent that he would put them on his gramophone again and again.[5]

Dorabella relates how on one occasion Elgar informed her of his intention to write a fantasy on a song called *Villikins and his Dinah*, which sounds very Stephen Fosterish.

Could it just be that somewhere or other there is a negro or Christy minstrel song which is the common ancestor of both the 'Enigma' theme and *Ol' Man River*? I've looked at forty or so Stephen Foster songs to no avail, but the possibility is still intriguing...

As a postscript, a tantalising little detail. Kern, as I have shown, would almost certainly have been familiar with Elgar's music. As it happens, Elgar, whilst not necessarily familiar with Kern's, at least knew *Ol' Man River*. Jerrold Northrop Moore tells of one night in 1928 when the Gramophone Company's artist manager, Trevor Osmond Williams, took Elgar to see... *Show Boat*.[6]

Notes

1. Bordman – p 29

2. Ibid – p 242

3. Freedland– p 90

4. Ibid– p 88

5. Reed – *Elgar as I knew him* – p 108

6. Moore – *Life* – p 777

Appendix 2

The 'friends pictured within'

For the sake of completeness I include here some brief notes on the subjects of Elgar's *Variations* – the 'friends pictured within' as he called them in his dedication. For more complete biographical details readers are referred to Percy Young's essay *Friends pictured within* published in *Elgar Studies* (ed. Monk).

Variation I (G minor – *Andante*)
C.A.E.   Caroline Alice Elgar (née Roberts) (1848–1920)
Elgar's wife. They met in 1886 when Alice started to come to Elgar for piano accompaniment lessons, and were married at Brompton Oratory in London in 1889. Alice, nine years older than Elgar, was clearly an immensely important influence on the composer, as can be seen from the fact that his first major work, the overture *Froissart*, dates from the year after their marriage, whilst his last, the Cello Concerto, was written the year before her death. Elgar survived his wife by fourteen years, but in spite of plans and sketches for an opera and a third symphony (the latter recently elaborated into a performing work by Anthony Payne), produced no really important work during this period.

Variation II (G minor – *Allegro*)
H.D.S-P.   Hew David Steuart Powell (1851–1924)
A talented amateur pianist who lived in London but regularly visited Malvern and took part in the activities of the music circle there. He first met Alice Elgar before her marriage. He participated in regular music-making all through the 1890s, both in London and Malvern, often

forming a trio with Elgar and Basil Nevinson (see Variation XII). A small point worth noting is that although in the score Elgar uses a hyphen between the initials 'S' and 'P', according to the records of Steuart Powell's Oxford College (Exeter) his name was in fact written without a hyphen.[1]

Variation III (G major – *Allegretto*)
R.B.T.   Richard Baxter Townshend (1846–1923)
Brother-in-law to W M Baker (see Variation IV), and a frequent visitor to his home at Hasfield Court in Gloucestershire, not far from Alice's parents' home. The Baker family had been friends of Alice before she knew Elgar, and this friendship continued unabated after her marriage, with the result that Elgar himself came to know all the family. In fact, no fewer than three of the variations are concerned with members of this family (III, IV and X). Townshend, 52 years old when the Variations were conceived, was the oldest of Elgar's subjects.

Variation IV (G minor – *Allegro di molto*)
W.M.B.   William Meath Baker (1858–1935)
Squire of Hasfield Court, where Elgar spent many happy times, in particular with Baker's three sons. This family was particularly kind and supportive to the Elgars. Baker himself was a keen climber with apparently various Alpine 'firsts' to his credit.

Variation V (C minor – *Moderato*)
R.P.A.   Richard Penrose Arnold (1856–1908)
Arnold, who lived in Worcester, was the son of the poet Matthew Arnold. He apparently became friendly with Elgar chiefly due to their games of golf.

Variation VI (C major – *Andantino*)
Ysobel   Isabel Fitton (1868–1936)
Elgar had known the Fitton family since his youth. For a time in the 1890s Elgar gave viola lessons to Isabel. When the Worcestershire Philharmonic Society was founded in 1897 with Elgar as conductor, Isabel was one of its two secretaries, the other being Winifred Norbury (see Variation IX). Elgar dedicated three works to members of the family: one to Isabel, one to one of her sisters, and one to her mother.

Variation VII (C major – *Presto*)
Troyte   Arthur Troyte Griffith (1864–1942)
Troyte was assistant in the Malvern architectural business of the brother of Basil Nevinson (see Variation XII) and Elgar appears to have met him first in 1897. The friendship quickly developed and became one of Elgar's closest and longest.

Variation VIII (G major – *Allegretto*)
W.N.   Winifred Norbury (1861–1938)
Like Isabel Fitton, Winifred Norbury came from a large family with musical daughters. Also like Isabel, Winifred was secretary to the Worcestershire Philharmonic. She was of enormous help to Elgar in various ways, notably in copying orchestral parts.

Variation IX (E flat major – *Adagio*)
Nimrod   August Johannes Jaeger (1860–1909)
German by birth, Jaeger came to England when he was eighteen and started to work for Novello in 1890, the same year that Elgar initiated his relationship with the firm. It is unclear exactly when the two men first met, but the first surviving correspondence dates from 1897. It is difficult to exaggerate Jaeger's role in Elgar's rise to eminence. As well as handling all the administrative details involved in the process of bringing a manuscript score into print, Jaeger was adviser, comforter

and friend to Elgar during a period in which the composer sorely needed the sort of support that Jaeger was able to provide. Of all the variations, 'Nimrod' is the only one that Elgar quoted in *The Music Makers* of 1912 and he did so at the words:

But on one man's soul it hath broken
A light that doth not depart;
And his look, or a word he hath spoken
Wrought flame in another man's heart.

Elgar sent some explanatory notes on the work to Ernest Newman and in them wrote an eloquent tribute to Jaeger, who had died three years earlier:

... amongst all the inept writing and wrangling about music his voice was clear, ennobling, sober and sane, and for his help and inspiration I make this acknowledgement.[2]

Variation X (G major – *Allegretto*)
Dorabella   Dora Penny (1874–1964)
In 1895, The Reverend Alfred Penny of Wolverhampton, a widower with one daughter, Dora, married W M Baker's eldest sister, thus involving them both in the Hasfield Court circle. It was later on that year, when the Elgars went to Wolverhampton to see Mary Baker and her new family, that Elgar first met Dorabella. The friendship quickly blossomed and Dorabella became a fairly frequent visitor to the Elgars, always eager to take part in whatever happened to be going on, whether it involved kite-flying or page-turning. At 24 years old when the Variations were conceived, she was the youngest of Elgar's subjects, and outlived all the rest, remaining for 22 years the last surviving 'variant'.

Variation XI (G minor – *Allegro di molto*)
G.R.S.   George Robertson Sinclair (1863–1917)
Sinclair was organist at Hereford Cathedral from 1889 up until his death in 1917 and so Elgar would have known him for some nine years

before the *Variations* were written. Elgar was a frequent visitor to Sinclair's house and it was there that he wrote his musical contributions in Sinclair's visitors' book – 'The Moods of Dan' – and it was also there that parts of some of his major works were written, notably *The Apostles*, (see Chapter 4)

Variation XII (G minor – *Andante*)
B.G.N.   Basil George Nevinson (1853–1908)
Like Hew Steuart Powell, Nevinson lived in London but was a frequent visitor to Malvern, where he and his cello took an active part in the local music-making. Elgar often used to use Nevinson's home as a base when in London.

Variation XIII (G major – *Moderato*)
***   Lady Mary Lygon (1869–1927)
Lady Mary, of Madresfield Court between Malvern and Worcester, was a very active figure in the musical world of the Malvern area, creating in 1896 the Madresfield Musical Competition at which Elgar acted as judge. She was also one of the leading supporters of the Worcestershire Philharmonic Society.

Variation XIV (G major – *Allegro*)
E.D.U.   Edward William Elgar (1857–1934)
Elgar considered this as the Finale rather than as a variation but he numbered it as number fourteen to avoid having thirteen variations (see his letter quoted on page 75) and so it is included here. The mood of the music is totally different from that of the opening theme, which, as we saw in an earlier chapter, can also be said to represent the composer, or more accurately his frame of mind at the time the theme occurred to him.

In his notes to accompany the pianola roll issue of the *Variations*, Elgar wrote that the work was:

written at a time when friends were dubious & generally discouraging...[3]

It is very difficult to reconcile this statement with what appears to have been unconditional support on all sides, spearheaded by Alice and Jaeger. Just two weeks before the 'Enigma' theme first sounded on Elgar's piano, a veritable delegation of friends, including four 'variants', had trooped up to Leeds from Malvern for the first performance of *Caractacus*, after which a lot of nice things were said.

The formation of the Worcestershire Philharmonic seems to have had more than a little to do with the desire on the part of some of Elgar's friends to encourage him.

Perhaps the following, part of a letter written to Elgar by his friend Nicholas Kilbum on 20 November 1898, can be taken as representative of what all Elgar's friends were telling him at that time:

> Not to go on would, it seems to me, be an offence even against the Gods themselves, to whom our cry of deprivation wd., in such a case, never cease to ascend. That you should, <u>when the spirit moves</u>, go forward in the highest hope & trust appears to me a command from the unseen, which to disregard wd. be very nearly wicked, for if ever a man's capacities clearly indicated his fitness & mission, you are he.[4]

Elgar's comment would appear to reveal more about his own insecurity than it does about the attitude of his friends.

* * * * *

It is interesting to reflect for a moment on Elgar's choice of friends for the *Variations*. In some ways it was a perilous exercise as those friends of his who were not included may well have felt left out or even offended. We have evidence of one instance of 'sour grapes' in Rosa Burley's comment, quoted in Chapter 3, to the effect that she was not a variation but the theme itself. And whilst in no way 'sour grapes', one can detect a hint of regret in Wulstan Atkins' book when he mentions that at one point Elgar considered his father as a possible variant:

> Even though my father did not in the end become a 'Variation', nevertheless his personality was to impress itself on Elgar musically, and Elgar did associate him with themes in the Pomp and Circumstance No 3, dedicated to him...[5]

For the truth is that Elgar had friends other than those depicted in the *Variations* who in various cases were closer and of longer standing than some of those included. Hubert Leicester, for instance, had known Elgar since they were boys at school together, and their friendship was to last right up until Elgar's death. Charles Buck was another old friend who had provided Elgar with warm affection and solace, and a welcome in his Yorkshire home since the 1880s.

In fact we know from Elgar's notes and sketches that he did contemplate other variants, notably Ivor Atkins and Nicholas Kilburn, but decided against their inclusion. This, it seems to me, is a clear indication that Elgar's criteria when deciding who should be included and who omitted, had little to do with who was a close friend and who not. His inspiration was purely musical, finding its expression through several people who happened to form part of his circle of acquaintances at that time, some of whom, Jaeger for example, were indeed close friends.

We know from the accounts of the evening when Elgar first played the theme of the *Variations* on his piano that his first thoughts went to instrumentalists – Hew Steuart Powell and Basil Nevinson, pianist and cellist respectively. Other sources of inspiration were habits or mannerisms capable of musical expression – William Baker's habit of slamming the door behind him and Richard Arnold's characteristic laugh. Jaeger's variation, 'Nimrod', recalls a conversation between Jaeger and Elgar during which the example of Beethoven was invoked by Jaeger as a source of encouragement for Elgar, and so the variation is reminiscent in its opening bars of the slow movement of Beethoven's *Pathétique* Sonata. Similarly, Lady Mary Lygon's forthcoming voyage to Australia was evoked by a quotation from Mendelssohn.

I can only conclude, therefore, that Elgar's criteria for selection was purely musical and that if Ivor Atkins, for example, was not included, it was simply because Elgar could not find any satisfying musical expression to justify his inclusion.

Notes

1. Letter to the author from Susan Marshall, Home Bursar, 31 Jan 1997

2. Moore – *Lifetime Letters* – p 249

3. Notes for the Aeolian Company's 'Duo-Art' pianola rolls of the Variations (1929)

4. Moore – *Lifetime Letters* – p 71

5. Atkins – p 38

Appendix 3

The Variations on record

Well, they may live.[1]

This comment on the *Variations* which Elgar reportedly made towards the end of his life, whilst typical of a certain pessimism with regard to the lasting attraction of his music, has turned out to be a monumental understatement as the score is Elgar's most widely loved and admired major orchestral work.

George Bernard Shaw wrote:

> ... when I heard the Variations (...)I sat up and said 'Whew!' I knew we had got it at last.[2]

The musicologist Sir Donald Tovey was of the opinion that:

> there is many an ambitious composer of brilliant and revolutionary reputation who ought to be (...) washed in its crystal-clear scoring until he learns the meaning of artistic economy and mastery.[3]

The admiration was international. The renowned German conductor Fritz Steinbach said in 1902:

> ... Elgar, as this work shows, is a real pioneer with a new technique in orchestration, combining entirely original effects with almost unique virtuosity.[4]

And this universal admiration has endured unchanged over the years. Even in France, a country for some reason not attracted in general to Elgar's music, a recent history of music says of it that it includes:

> ... quelques oeuvres superbes, comme les *Variations Enigma*[5]
> (some superb works, such as the *Enigma Variations*)

It is therefore not surprising that the work is far and away the most frequently recorded of the major works.

The very first recording of the *Variations* was made in 1920 with Elgar himself conducting. In the intervening 78 years, the work has been recorded a total of 75 times, according to information kindly provided to me by John Knowles, author of the 1985 discography *Elgar's Interpreters on Record* and the acknowledged expert on Elgar recordings. These include one brass-band version and the 1995 recording by Anthony Goldstone of the piano version played on Elgar's own Broadwood piano.

Whilst these figures are already impressive, if we consider the fact that up until 1948 the work had been recorded nine times, then clearly over the past 50 years a new record has been issued on average well over once a year, which is even more impressive. At one point in early 1990, the reviewer of the *Elgar Society Journal* had no fewer than five new versions to consider in the same review.

These records, which include live performances, have been the work of a wide variety of orchestras and conductors, although perhaps inevitably English conductors outnumber their foreign counterparts. That said, non-English conductors still account for over a third of all the recordings.

Of all conductors, three were particularly assiduous, namely John Barbirolli, Adrian Boult and Malcolm Sargent, each of whom has had no fewer than four different versions on record.

Just behind this group comes, surprisingly, Arturo Toscanini with three recorded versions, two of which were live performances. Andrew Davis has also recorded the work three times, whilst no fewer than eight conductors have recorded the work twice – Elgar himself, Henry Wood, Charles Groves, Charles Mackerras, Neville Marriner, Georg Solti, Yehudi Menuhin and André Previn.

As far as orchestras are concerned, the London Philharmonic Orchestra has participated in 11 recordings, followed by the London Symphony Orchestra with eight.

Apart from these recordings of the complete work, Variation IX ('Nimrod') has been separately issued over 30 times, including 17 brass band versions, seven organ versions and even a rendering by The King's Singers. None of the other variations has ever been issued separately, not even Variation X ('Dorabella'), which of all the variations, it will be remembered, Elgar thought was most suitable for separate use.

Returning to the complete recordings, various of these deserve special mention and foremost among these are Elgar's own recordings, which whilst having a disadvantage in terms of sound quality are nonetheless priceless testimony of the composer's reading of his own work. Elgar recognized very early on the potential value of recorded music and we are fortunate that he left us so much of his music recorded under his own direction, all of which has been issued on compact disc.

We are also fortunate that an apparently legendary interpretation of the *Variations* has survived on disc, that of Arturo Toscanini, for the great conductor refused to allow the original 78s to be issued when they were made as at that time he hated recording and everything connected with it. This performance, with the BBC Symphony Orchestra, recorded live at a concert in 1935, builds to an electrifying account of the Finale and one can easily share the enthusiasm of the audience reaction at the end. The distinguished English conductor Sir Landon Ronald was present at what he called Toscanini's 'magnificent performance' and he wrote to *The Times*:

This great conductor rendered the work exactly as Elgar intended, and the composer's idiom obviously has no secret for Toscanini. Some of the best performances I have ever heard were from the composer himself, but this one on Friday night last excelled, because Toscanini has a great genius for conducting and Elgar had not. (...) We had the Variations from Toscanini exactly as Elgar wished them played.. .[6]

Sir Malcolm Sargent was present at one of Toscanini's concerts in 1930 when the *Variations* were given:

...this performance was overwhelming to me and to the audience. Everyone, having recovered from the emotional impact, stood up and shouted, recalling Toscanini time after time. I walked the Thames Embankment until four in the morning.[7]

Toscanini had in fact been playing the work for all of 25 years before the performance of which Sargent speaks and he was to record it twice more, both times with the NBC Symphony Orchestra, nearly 25 years later in 1951 and 1954 (he died in January 1957).

He said of the *Variations*:

... it is lovely music and it must be alive.[8]

...which irresistably recalls a famous comment Elgar made in one of his early letters to Jaeger:

Now my music, such as it is, is alive, you say it has heart – I always say to my wife (over any piece or passage of my work that pleases me): 'if you cut that it would bleed!'[9]

Another foreign conductor who had a special affection for the *Variations* was Leopold Stokowski, who recorded the work with the Czech Philharmonic Orchestra in 1972.

In the case of Stokowski, however, we have rather more than his recording, as he wrote an eloquent letter to Elgar in 1929 which is worth quoting 'in extenso':

I have just been conducting your Variations in Philadelphia and New York, and feel I must thank you for such a profound and intense musical pleasure as I received from them. We had not played them for four seasons, and the impression I received from them was of such depth of feeling and beauty that I was stirred by this music far more profoundly than I can express in words. Often when we play a work after not having heard it for several seasons, we have the impression of its being the expression of another period and of its being alien to the life of today. But your Variations gave me the most powerful impression of eternal vitality and architectural design – and also of something very difficult to express, a floating upward into a mystical level where time and space seem to cease.[10]

Intriguingly, it would appear that Stokowski, who as a teenager first met Elgar at about the time the *Variations* were written, even had his own suggestion as to the 'real' identity behind the asterisks of Variation XIII[11], and Michael Kennedy has actually asserted that this suggestion was Helen Weaver[12]. However, I have been unable to trace the original source of Stokowski's comments.

Without any doubt the most controversial recording was Leonard Bernstein's with the BBC Symphony Orchestra on Deutsche Grammophon in 1982. Bernstein's highly idiosyncratic reading of the work involved choices of tempi which shocked some critics, and this is best illustrated in the 'Nimrod' variation, in which he takes the music at half the speed of everybody else. Indeed, the comparison with Elgar's second recording of 1926 is even more striking as whereas Elgar takes 2m 52s to play the variation, Bernstein takes 6m 12s!

It was even said that there was a minor revolution in the ranks of the BBCSO at such tempi, and the *Elgar Society Journal* reviewer, whilst not entirely damning in his comments, nonetheless ended his review thus:

> Bernstein will occupy a place of some distinction in 20th-century music. It is sad to think that this might be for the eccentricity rather than the integrity of his style. This recording demonstrates his finest and his worst qualities, the latter entirely to the detriment of his reputation.[13]

It is true that Bernstein takes 'Nimrod' very slowly, but it is equally true that Elgar himself, when he realized that in performance he was playing the variation slower than written, altered the original metronome marking to a slower speed and changed the direction from Moderato to Adagio. To a certain extent, then, Bernstein does nothing more than continue in the same direction that Elgar had initiated, although admittedly in an exaggerated manner. What is undoubtedly true is that the music loses nothing in grandeur in Bernstein's performance and his slow tempo in fact gives him more time to handle the transition from the climax of the variation to its quiet end which happens in the space of just two bars and which often appears rather abrupt in many other recordings.

At the end of the day, choosing a 'best buy' among all the recorded versions is an impossible task as so many good accounts have been recorded and so much depends on personal taste. For instance, there are those who prefer the Finale with the organ audible in all its splendour, whilst others would rather hear Elgar's magnificent orchestra with the organ taking a back seat (or indeed no seat at all as it is an optional part). The only certainty of any selection is, therefore, that it will inevitably upset somebody!

However, apart from Elgar and Toscanini already mentioned, my choice among older recordings would be three which remain landmarks in the recording history of this work, namely Pierre Monteux, Sir John Barbirolli in his version with the Hallé Orchestra in 1957, and Sir Thomas Beecham.

Among recent recordings (over the last ten years) I would single out Sir Simon Rattle, Bryden Thomson and Charles Dutoit (who carries on the tradition of fine performances by non-English conductors).

That gives me my eight choices for my desert island. But as each castaway is allowed an extra luxury, I would choose the recording which first introduced me to this music as a schoolboy and to which I invariably return, and that is Sir Malcolm Sargent's 1959 performance with the Philharmonia Orchestra.

Notes

1. quoted in Young – *Elgar OM* – p 278

2. *Music and Letters*, Vol.1 No. 1,1920 – Reprinted in Red wood – pp 245-250

3. *Essays in Musical Analysis* (1936) – quoted in Kennedy – Portrait – p 100

4. quoted in Young – *Elgar OM* – p 106

5. Roland de Candé – *Histoire Universelle de la Musique* – Seuil (1978) – Vol. 2 p 154

6. 6 June 1935. Quoted in ESJ – May 1990 – p 6

7. *Music & Musicians*, June 1957. Reprinted in Redwood – pp 162 –164

8. Quoted from Bernard Shore – *The Orchestra Speaks* – in CD notes by Tony Harrison (EMI 1987)

9. Moore – *Publishers' Letters* – p 49

10. Moore – *Lifetime Letters* – p 421

11. ESJ – Sept 1983 – p 25

12. Kennedy – *The Soul Enshrined: Elgar and his Violin Concerto* – p 76. Published in Monk (ed) – *Music and Literature*

13. ESJ – May 1993

Post Scriptum

1. *My website*

Since the book was first published, I have received a fair number of communications from a whole range of people around the world. I pulled together a number of these into a website that I entitled Post Scriptum, and I reproduce them here.

The original ending to the Finale

Chapter 5, p 97
...the original Finale has been abandoned...

A performance of the Variations by the Philharmonia Orchestra under Richard Hickox in Worcester Cathedral on 4 June 1999 used the original Finale.

A note in the July 1999 issue of the *Elgar Society News* reads: 'The chief item of interest was the use of the original ending to 'E.D.U.', played at the première in June 1899. In this the Coda is cut short, and to those familiar with the work it comes as a real shock and with a sense of deprivation! However, almost as an encore (though it was programmed beforehand) this was immediately followed by the longer version, which Jaeger had argued for, and which Elgar came to see was the correct peroration of the work.'

The original ending to the Finale (2)

In response to the previous point, I have received an e-mail from Joel Lazar, conductor of the JCC Symphony Orchestra in Maryland, USA.

He wrote as follows:

'The *Variations*' have fascinated me since my school days and I've heard many wonderful performances of them, including Monteux and the Boston Symphony in early 1964, the last concert he conducted before his death.'

Re your request for documentation of performances of the original ending, here's a 'close but not quite' case – The Maryland Symphony Orchestra [based in Hagerstown, Maryland, USA; originally conducted by Barry Tuckwell], performed a portion of the finale with the original ending as part of a pre-performance talk on Enigma by their current Music Director, Elizabeth Schultze, in the Fall of 1999. I'm sorry I can't be more specific; I was there, in fact, but I don't seem to have a copy of the program to hand. In the actual concert, of course, they performed the published ending.

Needless to say, I was shocked by the brevity of the original ending. I suppose I shouldn't have been; I'd seen it in the MS score on display at the British Museum on my first visit to London as far back as 1970, and of course seen it since in photographic reproduction. I must say it sounded even worse than it looked!

Elgar's standard reply to 'enigma solvers'

Chapter 6, p 107
Elgar's death in 1934 obviously removed the possibility of would-be enigma solvers trying their attempts directly on the composer himself.

A letter from Raymond Monk published in the July 1999 issue of the *Elgar Society Journal* gives me the opportunity to mention another book on the *'Enigma' Variations* also published in 1999. This is *Elgar 'Enigma' Variations* by Julian Rushton, West Riding Professor of Music at the University of Leeds. The book was published by Cambridge University Press.

Raymond Monk's very kind letter reads as follows:

'Julian Rushton and Patrick Turner with their notable* additions to the Elgar bibliography have celebrated the *Enigma* centenary in fine style. Both books are a joy to read and I for one will be returning to them again and again. However, those who would embark on Enigma puzzle-solving in the next century may like to read Elgar's standard reply to those 'solutions' which appeared during his lifetime:

Severn House, Hampstead, NW.

<u>No</u>: *nothing like it.*
I do not see that the tune you suggest fits in the least.
E.E.
And I am inclined to the view that all subsequent attempts would have met with this same response!'

* corrected from the originally published 'noble' following information received from Geoffrey Hodgkins, Editor of the *Elgar Society Journal.*

Hans Richter and the Vienna Opera

Chapter 1, p 33
...having previously been in charge of the Vienna Philharmonic Orchestra (and thus Musical Director of the Vienna Opera)...

Christopher Fifield wrote to me as follows: '...in fact he never held such a position. He didn't want to be Musical Director of any opera house after his experience of such a post in Budapest in the early 1870s. He went to Vienna in 1875 specifically as Erste (first) Kapellmeister, with Franz Jauner (a theatre administrator) and then Wilhelm Jahn (a conductor) above him in the post of General Director. Naturally Richter overshadowed both of them but in Jahn's case their repertoire tastes complemented one another's and Jahn did most of the Italian operas. When Mahler arrived as Music Director problems arose as he wanted to do Wagner, and by then Richter was tired and quite prepared to take his pension and emigrate to Manchester in 1900.'

In his letter, Christopher mentions another point connected with the *'Enigma' Variations*, also involving Richter: '....one of the Richter descendants kindly gave me a leather-bound miniature score of the *Variations*. In it, Elgar has inscribed the following:

I send the first copy of this miniature score. Yrs. EE

To Hans Richter: true Artist and true Friend from Edward Elgar: March 1904. Do not let the lessened size of this score, which you first presented to an audience, lessen your regard for the music or your love for me! EE

In other words, the dedication to Richter so often associated with Elgar's 1st symphony of 1908 was used four years earlier at the time of the Covent Garden Festival, a three-day event devoted to Elgar's music and organised for him by Richter, a terrific accolade by the conductor to the composer. Richter always said at the end of his life that for him there had only been two musical gods, Wagner and Elgar.'

Christopher Fifield, conductor and writer, is author of *True Artist and True Friend, a Biography of Hans Richter* (OUP Clarendon Press 1993)

Mozart's Prague Symphony

Chapter 6, p 108 (list of previous solutions)
1977   Prague Symphony (Mozart)   J M Nosworthy

In his letter referred to above, Christopher Fifield also writes the following: '...in about the same year (1977) I bought a number of Mozart symphonies in full score published by Breitkopf and Hartel in a second hand music shop as I was building up my collection of working scores as a conductor. In the slow movement a previous owner (a conductor I believe) had written in pencil 'Elgar Enigma Variations?' at both points where the striking likeness occurs. Judging by the style of handwriting it was written many years earlier, so the idea of the *Prague* Symphony predates 1977 by a long way in my view.'

As I point out in the book, my list of previously suggested solutions records their first mention in print somewhere, and J M Nosworthy's letter to *The Daily Telegraph* was the earliest published mention of it I could find.

Christopher makes another point related to Mozart's symphony: 'Above all, how did the *Prague* Symphony come to be played at the end of the concert on 19 June 1899 because I'm sure Elgar would not have had the presumption to ask Richter, so did the conductor put it in because he was reminded of the symphony when he read Elgar's MS?

All very intriguing......'

Locked-away envelopes...

Chapter 8, p 119
...unless the explanation is in an envelope locked away in some lawyer's safe somewhere...

I have learned that there is, in fact, such an envelope, not in some lawyer's safe, but in the safekeeping of the Elgar Birthplace museum at Broadheath.

According to Chris Bennett of the Birthplace museum, there are instructions that this envelope is only to be opened 100 years after Elgar's death (which will be in 2034). He added that it would seem from the little that is known about the envelope that its contents have something to do with *The Dream of Gerontius*.

Although this would appear to squash any hopes that it might contain the solution to the enigma, the very fact that it exists shows that the idea of such an envelope is not so fanciful as it might seem.

2. *Subsequent articles*

Interest in the *'Enigma' Variations* has by no means dimmed since my book was first published, and indeed, the November 2004 edition of the *Elgar Society Journal* carried no fewer than three articles on the subject of the 'hidden theme'. Two of these involved ciphers.

Andrew Moodie suggested that Elgar had enciphered Carice, his daughter's name, in musical notation, using the letter/note equivalents often used by composers. The name 'Carice', enciphered musically in this way would give the note sequence CADBCE. Mr Moodie showed that all six notes occur in the 'Enigma' theme, although not in that exact sequence, and this, for him, was enough to propose the cipher as the solution to the enigma.

However, there are problems with this. For example, finding six out of the eight notes in the scale in the theme doesn't seem to me to be particularly significant, all the more so as Mr Moodie has to resort to some pretty convoluted reasoning in order to 'find' them, for example –

...bar 4 contains a G which cannot be derived from the notes CADBCE of 'Carice' without some reorganisation. An inversion of CADBCE gives ACGBAC, and the notes 3, 5, 4 and 6 of this inversion produce the notes GABC of bar 4.

As he himself says, 'I doubt that Elgar would have gone to these lengths'.

Stephen Pickett also suggested a cipher, this time linking the initials and names of the 'variants' with the 13 letters that make up the name of the song 'Rule Britannia', thus providing a new rationale for the solution originally proposed by Theodore van Houten.

Edmund M Green proposes a solution in a totally different direction – Shakespeare's Sonnets, and in particular Sonnet 66. Mr Green proposes that in each of this sonnet's 14 lines there are words that suggest all of the 'variants' as described in *My Friends Pictured Within*, Elgar's description of his 'variants' first published in 1928. For example, the words 'behold desert' in line 2 are said to suggest Elgar's phrase 'chromatic beyond H.D.S-P.'s liking' describing Variation 11; and the words 'trimmed in jollity' in line 3 supposedly reflect 'presentation of an old man in some amateur theatricals', in Elgar's description of R.B.T.

It seems to me that whilst undoubtedly ingenious, all three 'solutions' fall into the 'hopelessly far-fetched' category, not only because of the tortuous mental convolutions required by each one, but because all of them pre-suppose a deliberately created puzzle on Elgar's part, something that I am convinced did not exist (see Chapter 1).

More recently, the July and November 2005 editions of the *Elgar Society Journal* published a long and painstakingly researched piece by Ernest Blamires on the identity behind the three asterisks of Variation 13. Mr Blamires comes down squarely behind the Helen Weaver theory, and he does so largely because of careful research into the movements of Lady Mary Lygon. The main thrust behind his argument centres around two apparently contradictory facts –

1 Elgar's statement quoted on p69 to the effect that at the time of writing the variation, its subject was on a long sea voyage
2. the fact that the music had already been written by the time Elgar learned of Lady Mary's impending departure to Australia.

However, one of the items of evidence that he cites is a letter that Lady Mary wrote to her brother the day after her visit to the Elgars on 21st February 1899 –

He (ie, Elgar) has written some big orchestra theme & variations - & each of the latter portrays a friend. I am one called 'Incognita' but I only heard this today – as he was too shy to tell me - & would not play them...

Even though this would seem to offer additional evidence in favour of Lady Mary, Mr Blamires still manages to argue that in reality Elgar was using her as a sort of front to conceal the identity of Helen Weaver.

I have to say that, much though I admire Mr Blamires's excellent article, I still hold to the opinion I expressed in Chapter 4, that is that although it seems to me perfectly possible that memories of Helen spilled over into this variation, it was still primarily intended as LML's.

3. *The Variations on record*

The rate at which new recordings have been added to the catalogue has continued at the rate of more than one every year since the book was published, with nine new versions issued, two of them of the piano version. One of the new orchestral versions was, in fact, a DVD recorded live in Worcester Cathedral by Sir Andrew Davis and the BBC

SO, as part of a documentary featuring the work and its background. This was Sir Andrew's fourth recording of the work which draws him level with Barbirolli, Boult and Sargent in the group of conductors with most recordings to their name.[1]

One particularly noteworthy addition to the catalogue is the 2003 recording by the Hallé Orchestra under Mark Elder. This CD is the first ever to have the orchestral version of the original ending, added as an extra item at the end of the disk.

4. *Twinkle twinkle little star*

The solution that I proposed to the Enigma, ie, Twinkle Twinkle Little Star, was treated kindly on the whole, despite some scoffs and giggles here and there.

The *Classical Music* reviewer in July 1999 said –

I remain convinced at a purely musical level that Turner's solution fits better than so many solutions put forward over the years.

Robert Anderson, writing in the *Elgar Society Journal* of March 1999, had this to say –

I have enjoyed playing the relevant six bars on the piano, grimacing slightly at the clashes, but thinking feelingly about Elgar at The Mount on 21 October 1898 maybe suffering as many child violinists on that particular tune as conscientious Suzuki mothers must endure today.

The 'fit' was even tested out on the piano in the 2004 BBC television documentary mentioned in the preceding section in which Sir Andrew Davis explored the background to the work. Sir Andrew was dismissive of my solution, and failed to acknowledge its parenthood, but it is impossible for me not to feel satisfaction that he singled it out for mention.

---

[1] I am grateful for this information to John Knowles, author of the 1985 discography *Elgar's Interpreters on Record*, and acknowledged expert in the field.

My own view has not changed since the book was first published. If I had to change anything in the case I make, it would be to take some emphasis away from the direct TTLS – Enigma theme match, and add more to what I strongly believe was the sequence of events –

1. TTLS in Elgar's mind after a long and depressing day's violin teaching
2. his playing of a series of chords harmonising with the tune in the minor key, very much like an improvisation of an experienced organist, which Elgar was.
3. the Enigma theme emerging as a counterpoint to those chords in the manner of a passacaglia.

Bibliography

e following list of writings on Elgar does not pretend to be exhaustive but
nply gives details of books and articles I have referred to in the text and
pecially in the notes at the end of each chapter.

KINS, Wulstan. *The Elgar-Atkins Friendship.* David and Charles 1984

ADES, James. *Orchestral Percussion Technique.* OUP 1961

RDMAN, Gerald. *Jerome Kern: His Life and Music.* OUP 1990

CKLEY, R J. *Sir Edward Elgar.* John Lane 1905

RLEY, Rosa / CARRUTHERS Frank C. *Edward Elgar: the Record of a
   Friendship.* Barrie & Jenkins 1972

E-LA-NOY, Michael. *Elgar the Man.* Allen Lane 1983

UNHILL, T F. *Sir Edward Elgar.* Blackie 1938

RSYTH, J A. 'Edward Elgar:True Artist and True Friend'.
   The Music Student, Dec 1932

REEDLAND, Michael. *Jerome Kern: A Biography.* Robson Books 1978

ENNEDY, Michael. *Portrait of Elgar.* OUP 1982

ENNEDY, Michael. *Elgar Orchestral Music.* BBC Publications 1970

NOWLES, John. *Elgar's Interpreters on Record.* Thames 1985

AINE, Basil. Elgar: his Life and Works. Bell and Sons 1933

ENUHIN, Yehudi. *Voyage Inachevé. Seuil* 1977

ONK, Raymond (ed). Elgar Studies. Scolar Press 1990

ONK, Raymond (ed). *Edward Elgar: Music and Literature.*
   Scolar Press 1993

OORE, Jerrold Northrop. *Edward Elgar: A Creative Life.* OUP 1984

OORE, Jerrold Northrop. *Spirit of England.* Heinemann 1984

OORE, Jerrold Northrop. *Elgar and his Publishers.* OUP 1987

OORE, Jerrold Northrop. *Edward Elgar: Letters of a Lifetime.* OUP 1990

EWMAN, Ernest. *Elgar.* John Lane 1906

PARROTT, Ian. *Elgar.* J M Dent 1971

POWELL, Mrs Richard. *Memories of a Variation.* Remploy 1979

REDWOOD, Christopher (ed). *An Elgar Companion.* Sequoia Publ. 1982

REED, W H. *Elgar.* J M Dent 1943

REED, W H. *Elgar as I Knew Him.* Gollancz 1973

WOOD, Henry J. *My Life of Music.* Gollancz 1938

YOUNG, Percy. *Elgar O.M..* Greenwood Press 1980

YOUNG, Percy. *Letters of Edward Elgar.* Geoffrey Bles 1956

YOUNG, Percy. *Letters to Nimrod.* Dennis Dobson 1965

Index of Names

Index of Other Elgar Works

Printed in the United Kingdom by
Lightning Source UK Ltd., Milton Keynes
139152UK00001B/50/A